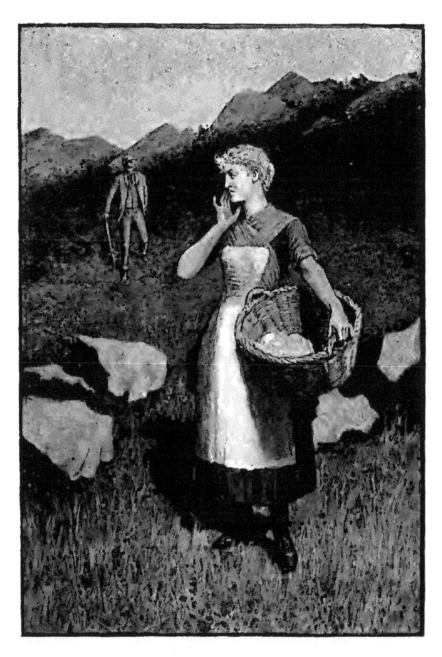

ON THE HILL-SIDE. [*Page* 137.

NABOTH'S VINEYARD

A Novel

BY

E. Œ. SOMERVILLE

AND

MARTIN ROSS

AUTHORS OF ' AN IRISH COUSIN '

LONDON

SPENCER BLACKETT

35, ST. BRIDE STREET, LUDGATE CIRCUS, E.C.

1891

CONTENTS.

vi   *CONTENTS.*

NABOTH'S VINEYARD.

CHAPTER I.

A SEASIDE HOTEL.

ANYONE who has glanced even cursorily at
the map of Ireland, will have noticed how
the south-west corner of it has suffered from
being the furthest outpost of European re-
sistance to the Atlantic. Winter after winter
the fight between sea and rock has raged on,
and now, after all these centuries of warfare,
the ragged fringe of points and headlands,
with long, winding inlets between them, look
as though some hungry monster's sharp teeth

I

had torn the soft, green land away, gnawing
it out from between the uncompromising
lines of rock that stand firm, indigestible
and undefeated.

Violent and unlovely though the usurp-
ing process may sound, the results, as is often
the case, justify the usurper.   Deep among
the hills the sea has forced its way, and, in
many quiet fiords, has settled itself down to
country life, surrounded by all sweet inland
sounds and sights, as serenely as if it had
never tossed the *City of Rome* about like a
shuttlecock, or climbed the tall Fastnet lighthouse till its light looked out through green
water.

Near the junction of the counties of Cork
and Kerry there is one of these fiords, where
everything has combined to help the sea in
its masquerade of freshwater simplicity : a
long island lies across its mouth, blocking the
wide south-western horizon, and almost join-

ing the two arms of land that stretch to meet each other on either side. Within them the green-blue water spreads itself in no bad imitation of a lake, till about a mile from the entrance, when the land closes in upon it, and the channel takes a sudden sharp twist to the north, and from that point runs like a river between hills that rise steeply from its narrowing curves, and are covered with thick woods that crowd to the water's edge, and trail their branches over the gray rocks and yellow seaweed.

The last thing that can be imputed to Irish architects of the beginning of this century is a wilful pandering to the picturesque, to the neglect of practical qualities. The little fishing town of Rossbrin was not built with the idea of adding to the beauties of Trahartha Harbour; it was simply a fortunate chance that the exigencies of shelter and anchorage had given it its position midway

between the open sea and the wooded bend
before mentioned. It had probably begun
with the battered row of fishermen's cottages
just above high-water mark, now almost
elbowed out of existence by a large ugly
building dominating the pier, with the
legend 'O'Grady's Stores' painted in black
letters on its gray walls. Following their
lead, other cottages have perched themselves
one above the other right up the face of the
hill, till anyone standing at the head of the
nearly perpendicular lane, that persevering
house-builders have compelled to pose as a
street, can see the gleaming slate roofs below
him, like an irregular flight of shining steps.
Two tall sycamores, outposts from the Trahartha woods, stand in the middle of the
street at the foot of the hill, which arches so
suddenly above them that the dwellers in the
houses half-way up can almost see into the
rooks' nests in their topmost branches.

These trees—'the Two Trees,' as they are
affectionately specialized by the people of
Rossbrin—are the recognised centre whence
radiates all the gossip of the place. They
have the effect of growing out of the middle
of a great cairn of stones, on the top of
which, according to tradition, the stocks once
held honourable position, and it is possible
that hereditary habit has something to say to
the invariable, almost helpless way in which
the male population of the place drift con-
gregationally into their shadow for purposes
of discussion and tobacco. Not till the top
of the hill is reached does Rossbrin begin to
expand and assert itself as one of the most
notable of the fishing villages of the south-
west. Here, in the three streets that detach
themselves from the central one, are the
post-office, the dispensary, the small but
refined establishment of ' Millinery in all its
branches,' kept by Miss Katty Vickery,

arbiter of modes and manners in Rossbrin;
the grocer's shop, where hob-nailed boots,
sickles, and coils of rope hang from the
ceiling, leaving little space for the more
legitimate occupancy of flitches of bacon and
bundles of dipped candles suspended by
their long wicks; and here, most imposing
of all, stands Donovan's Hotel, a species of
glorified public-house, its green and gold
signboard showing to great advantage on
its pink-washed wall. In spite of its gilded
assumption of hotel rank, its proprietor was
well aware that a larger part of his income
came to him across the counter of the public-
house than he derived from the more elegant
department upstairs; but it is doubtful if he
would have admitted as much to any of the
numerous rival publicans of Rossbrin; and
his wife, a young lady with a high standard
of gentility, went so far as to ignore the
public-house altogether, except when neces-

sity compelled her slightingly to refer to 'the bar.'

On a certain fine October afternoon in the year 1883, Mr. John Donovan himself might have been seen at a railed-in desk at the end of the bar counter, taking advantage of the slack business of the early afternoon hours to make up his books. His fat finger travelled rapidly up and down the columns, and every now and then from between his thick lips came a sibilant murmur of multiplication and addition. A large tin box stood open on a high stool beside him, and at frequent intervals he turned towards it, and, putting his pen in his mouth, took bundles of papers from it, and compared their contents with the entries in his book. It seemed a complicated system of accounts for either a hotel or a public-house, the items requiring constant reference to the most unexpected documents, such as leases, dirty I.O.U.'s, and

what appeared to be inventories of farm
stock, with pencilled notes and erasures.
He was not a good-looking man, this
wealthy Mr. John Donovan ; not even a
pleasant-looking one, with his dull brown
eyes set high over a cocked nose, and his
heavy cheeks showing through a sparsely-
growing black beard ; and when after a time
he stood up, his coarse, high-shouldered
figure was as unattractive as his face.

A sound of leisurely wheels in the road
made him look out through the open door,
and, with a glance at the clock, he locked
and put away his tin box, and took down his
hat from a peg over his head ; then, opening
a door into the back regions, he called in a
high, husky voice to a certain Joanna to
come and ' mind the shop,' and stepped
into the street.   There was waiting there
for him a low two-wheeled trap, the Irish
equivalent for a farmer's gig, with a dingy,

ewe-necked black mare in the shafts, who looked round at her proprietor with an expression of resentful melancholy as he took the reins from the boy who had been holding her, and got heavily into the trap. ·

'See here, Michael,' he said to the boy. 'Did Mr. O'Grady come up the street yet ?'

'He did. not, surr I think, for the fish steamer didn't go yit.'

'Well, as soon as she's gone he'll be coming up to see me, and let you be looking out for him, and tell him not to leave the town till I come back. Tell him I've business beyond in Scariff.'

The chuck at the bit, which the mare had been anticipating, followed the words, and Mr. Donovan drove away up the street, eyeing the loungers at the shop-doors with an air of disapproving hauteur that was only becoming in a man who was owed money by a large proportion of the inhabitants. Perhaps, if he had condescended so far as to look behind him, it might have occurred to him that the interest with which they in their turn regarded his broad, prosperous back and slouching shoulders, as he drove away from them, was not quite as gratifying as that which he received periodically in large and small amounts across his counter, though it did not require at all the same amount of stimulation. But Mr. Donovan seldom looked behind him in any sense; his attention was altogether given to a future more or less expansive—one, in fact, limited only by a point that, distant though it was, still required to be perpetually moved on—the point up to which he felt his financial position quite assured.

The shambling trot which the mare's self-respect had induced her to maintain through the town settled down into a resigned plod-

ding as her owner's ponderous hand turned
her out of the street, and into a hilly road
that bent away inland, following the high
demesne wall that screened the outlook over
the Trahartha woods eastward to the open
sea.   For about a quarter of a mile the gray
forbidding wall stretched without a break or
so much as a trail of ivy to soften its severity,
an obstacle all the more depressing to the
wayfarer from the knowledge of what it was
hiding from him; but if custom had left to
Mr. Donovan a conscious opinion on the
subject, it would have been respectful admiration for the amount of money it represented,
and for its small-boy resisting power.   At
the top of the long hill from Rossbrin, there
was a break in its implacable monotony, and
between the pillars of a tall iron gate came a
dazzle of bright colour.   A broad sunny
stretch of grass sloped away, broken by
clumps of elms that shone golden in the level

afternoon sun, to the great mass of the
woods ; and above all hung the high sea line,
with a lighthouse, poised like a white gull
between the two blues of sea and sky. The
mare's stout sides were heaving as she
reached the flat ground opposite the gateway,
but it was neither compassion for her, nor
any feeling of pleasure in the suddenly dis-
closed view, that induced Mr. Donovan to
bring her laboured crawl to a standstill.
He had caught a glimpse between the trees
of the park of a woman walking quickly over
the grass towards the gate. She was still
some little way off, and he sat waiting there
patiently till she should come within earshot.
His eyes, from under their thick hanging lids,
were concentrated on her, with an expression
that made his dull face almost fervid, and
revealed a fact that his most intimate friends
hardly suspected ; though to the woman now
nearing the gate, the knowledge that John

Donovan was in love with his wife was a sufficiently old story.

' Why, Harriet, where were ye ?' he called out to her. ' I thought ye were below in the town.'

She did not answer till she was near enough to speak without raising her voice.

'What'd keep me in the town ?' she replied ungraciously. ' I came up here to get out of the smell of them beastly fish !'

She was a tall, strongly-built young woman of, perhaps, thirty, pale-faced, with strong black brows that gave emphasis to the restless, stormy dark eyes beneath them. She was distinctly handsome, although the lower part of her face was disproportionately large, and the underlip projected discontentedly, contradicting the generous and somewhat sensuous expression of her large full-lipped mouth.

' Well, indeed, the air'd be heartier like for ye up here,' said Donovan conciliatingly.

'Any way, we'll be done with this lot soon; I hear Rick O'Grady's steamer is for starting this afternoon.'

'She's going now,' Harriet answered. 'I seen her getting up steam awhile ago. There she is, in the harbour's mouth.'

She turned and pointed to a dark stream of smoke, which just showed above the yellow tree tops. Her husband's eyes contracted suspiciously.

'And is it home you're going now?' he asked; then, without waiting for her reply: 'Wouldn't it be as good for ye to come on with me to the Widow Leonard's?'

She swung her cheap black-handled umbrella to and fro, with her eyes fixed on the ground, as if in uncertainty. Then she flung a glance up at her husband's face, as he bent a little towards her.

'No; I don't want to go see them Leonards,' she said, with the undercurrent of ill-humour in her voice rather more pronounced than before; ' I'm going back home now.' She closed the gate behind her and turned in the direction of Ross-brin.

Donovan knew that set of Harriet's under-lip, with its accompanying lift of the chin, and judiciously abandoned a losing game. He was a man not in the habit of betraying his feelings, and the mare was the only one qualified to argue, from the unusually heavy blow with which she was again started on her journey, that Donovan had any dislike to his wife's returning to a *tête-à-tête* with Mr. Richard O'Grady.

CHAPTER II.

UNWRITTEN LAW.

It was mentioned, a few pages back, that Trahartha Harbour curved sharply from its original course inland; but the geographical crudities of a first description are seldom sufficiently laid to heart by the reader, and the purposes of this story make it, unhappily, necessary to compel the attention to these uninteresting details.

After that sudden and most graceful curve, the harbour spreads itself into an excellent imitation of a lake, and then stretches a long narrow arm westward to meet the little Rowrie River, that runs a fierce course from

its mother lake, four miles back in the bogs
of Corran, where wild-geese are seen in the
hard winters, and the pike are said to be of
antediluvian age and size. The road which
Mr. Donovan was now taking made a long
loop round the Trahartha woods, and cross-
ing the river by a respectable stone bridge,
about half a mile from its mouth, struck into
the desolate hilly country north of the harbour.
The Widow Leonard's farm lay between this
bridge and the head of the harbour, and the
bohireen which led to it from the main road
was stony enough to have materially loosened
Mr. Donovan's hold over his temper by the
time he arrived at the farmyard. The bent
and rusty iron gate stood hospitably open, and
a fine flock of geese who were solemnly stalk-
ing forth to a muddy pond at the other side
of the bohireen were thrown into sudden confusion by the mare and trap, and hurried, with
hysterical screechings, back to the manure-

2

heap which graced the centre of the farmyard.
This was, as is common in the South of
Ireland, a small square, two sides of which
were formed by untidy thatched farm-build-
ings, and the third and fourth by the furze-
topped fence in which the gate was, and by
the house. In front of the latter stood its proprietor, a big bony woman of about fifty, with
wavy grizzled hair and a startlingly red face.
Her entire appearance was determined and
even truculent, and just at this moment its
effect was much enhanced by the energy with
which she was lifting wet coils of linen from
a washing-tub, and shaking them out with
detonating flaps, before hanging them on the
line strained from the top rail of the open gate
to a conveniently stripped rafter of the pigsty.

'Good-evening to ye, Misther Donovan,'
she said, in a voice that lent added violence
to the loud, argumentative Southern brogue.
She took from between her teeth a large

brass pin, which slightly thickened her utterance, and spearing through a thick flannel
petticoat with it, immediately addressed herself, as usual, to the topic uppermost in her
mind : ' Nothing would sarve that brayching
little robber of a red heifer but to ate the tail
out of me new petticoat ! Faith, I knew by
her she was watching me spreadin' it above
on the bushes ; but she's that 'cute, she never
came next nor nigh it till she got me
within in the house, and I never felt her then
till she had it ate. Faith ! it's up this night
into Dhrimnahoon she'll go. Maybe she
won't lep them walls so handy, for as clever
as she is !'

During this address, Donovan had got out
of his trap, and he stood waiting in silence
till it was ended.

' I think ye'd do well, Mrs. Leonard,' he
said slowly, ' to send no more cattle out to
Drimnahoon.'

Mrs. Leonard checked herself abruptly in the act of shaking out a towel.

'And for why?' she demanded, in a voice loud enough to have been heard three fields off.

Donovan looked all round the farmyard before he answered. There was nothing to be heard or seen except the pigs, eating noisily and disgustingly in their sty, the geese standing thoughtfully about on the top of the manure-heap, and a few calves waiting for their evening refection. But Donovan's slow, observant eye penetrated the cavernous darkness of the cowshed, and discovered there the figure of a man standing, pitchfork in hand, in the dried bracken that he had been shaking out for litter when the conversation outside had attracted his attention.

'The evening's turning a trifle cold,' observed the hotel-keeper, as if Mrs. Leonard had not spoken. 'If it's agree'ble to ye, I'll

step inside to the fire. Here, Dan,' he called;
'come out and put a hand to the mare for
awhile.'

The man in the cowhouse put down his
fork, and slouching across the slushy yard
without looking at Donovan, took up his
position at the mare's head. In the distance
his strong rounded shoulders and thickset
figure had made him appear a middle-aged
man, so that it was almost startling to see
that his face was that of a sullen, ugly young
fellow of two or three and twenty : in colour
a brickdust pink ; in shape, a pudding that
has defied the restraining influences of the
pudding-cloth ; in general effect, a remarkable
confirmation of the theory that those who
live on potatoes finally acquire a likeness to
that vegetable. Perhaps the strangest thing
about Dan Hurley's looks was the thatch of
pale hair that hung to his eyes in front, and
nearly touched the collar of his flannel jacket

behind. It was almost white, and, con-
trasting with the darker tone of his face,
gave his light eyes an unnatural stare and
prominence.

Donovan's eye rested on him with dis-
favour, and as he followed Mrs. Leonard into
the house he said, loud enough to be heard
by Dan :

'If that was my servant-boy I'd learn him
the manners to put his hand tc his hat when
he's spoke to by his betthers.'

'His manners is good enough for me,'
responded Mrs. Leonard, with a sound in
her voice indicative of a gathering storm.
She dragged forward a chair for her guest,
and then, addressing herself to a big pot of
cabbage, that was bubbling over the turf fire
and blocking its friendly blaze, she hoisted
it off its hook and set it down on the earthen
floor with a thump. The demands of politeness to a visitor had been fulfilled.

'And now maybe ye'll tell me what's this ye're sayin' to me about Dhrimnahoon,' she said.

Donovan settled himself in his chair, and cleared his throat impressively.

'Well, Mrs. Leonard,' he began with a moderation born of superiority, 'I don't doubt but ye'll remember the surkumstances that was taking place on that farm of Drim- nahoon all these months back. You know very well the way poor James Mahony had to quit out of it, because he couldn't pay the rack-rent, and the risolewtions that the League passed in regard of it——'

Mrs. Leonard had been stooping over the pot, stirring and breaking up the cabbage in it, while Donovan spoke, but at this point she straightened herself up.

'There's no one need come here to tell me about the Land Laygue!' she shouted; 'I'm as good a mimber as there is in it. I pay

my dues regular, and I thank my God I'm
able to do it, and no thanks to annyone in the
counthry !'

Whenever Mrs. Leonard thanked her God
in this aggressive manner it might safely be
assumed that her temper and her self-esteem
had risen to boiling-point. She stood with
the steaming pot-stick clenched in her right
hand, and glared at Donovan through the
fumes of the cabbage.

' There's no one disputin' ye're not a good
Leaguer, Mrs. Leonard,' he said with the
same exasperating suavity ; ' and that was
what was surprisin' us that you'd be the one
to take a farm that was boycotted by ordhers
from Head Quarthers.'

' An' didn't me own mother's brother have
that land before Jamesy Mahony took it ?'
replied Mrs. Leonard, still in the high key of
righteous indignation ; ' an' I never thought
to take it till I heard Tom Carey was applyin'

for it—him that's the landlords' man and never ped a penny to the Laygue—"an sure," says I, "isn't it betther a good Layguer should have it than the likes of him ?"'

Donovan rose to his feet and let his cold fishy eye rest on her excited face.

'Ye'll please to take notice now,' he said, 'that as President of the Rossbrin Branch, I have inforrmed you that the ordhers of the League is that you give up the farm of Drimnahoon. And as a friend I may tell ye that we cannot be responsible if outrages occurs. There is them in this counthry that cares nayther for the Law nor the League, so long as they'll get quit of land-grabbers. 'Tisn't so long since Captain Moonlight was heard of hereabouts.'

'To the divil I pitch Captain Moonlight!' retorted Mrs. Leonard unhesitatingly, with defiant arms akimbo ; 'and my answer to the

Laygue is that when I give over payin' me
subscription it'll be time for them to be givin'
me their ordhers about me own uncle's land;
but as long as I'm payin' regular there's no
one has any call to intherfare with me!'

She received no answer. Donovan was
already half-way to the door, his face showing
no irritation or wish to prove his case. This
departure in silence was the most effective he
could possibly have chosen, a fact of which
he was well aware, so it was especially an-
noying that just as he reached the door it
was flung open in his face and a heavy can
of milk was set down at his very feet, blocking his exit and surprising him into an un-
dignified backwards start.

'Who's that? Can't ye mind where ye're
comin' l' he said sharply; then recognising
Dan in the dark entry: 'What the devil
business had you to leave the mare?'

' It was carryin' in the can of milk he was

for me, Misther Donovan,' replied a girl's voice apologetically.

' 'Twould be betther for him to do as he's bid,' replied Donovan, shouldering past Dan into the yard.

' And what call had he to obey your ordhers more than my daughther's ?' screamed the widow from within, hurrying forth to do battle. ' It's you he may thank that he's a sarvant-boy this day, an' he knows that well ! A grand Land Layguer ye are to be talkin' to me about Dhrimnahoon, an' you fattening yer bastes on the land that was his mother's till ye dhruv her to the workhouse !'

' Ah, whisht, mother !' said the girl, who seemed to hold Donovan in far more awe than did her stalwart parent. ' I'm very sorry, Misther Donovan. I thought the horse would stand.'

This fact was at the moment self-evident, the mare's head being drooped between her

knees in a sluggish doze ; but Donovan disregarded the apology. He climbed into his
trap, and then, as he slowly dragged the
mare's head round towards the gate, he turned
to Ellen Leonard.

'Maybe ye've more sense than your
mother, and if ye have I tell ye it'll be the
best of your play to make her mind what I'm
afther sayin' to her about that farm of Drimnahoon.'

CHAPTER III.

MRS. DONOVAN AT HOME.

THE fish-steamer had slowly and cautiously picked her way through her little fleet of satellites, the brown-sailed fishing boats, and had disappeared round the eastern point of the harbour with her cargo of tightly-packed fish-barrels. The dark breath from her funnel smeared the faint rose-colour of the sky, and the foam of her wake still swam on the smooth ripples round the smart yellow punt in which Rick O'Grady was pulling himself ashore. He rowed fast; the October air was fresh and sharp, and he had been for several hours watching the slow stowing of

his fish-barrels in the steamer's hold, so that
the exertion was pleasant to him. Everything seemed pleasant to him this afternoon,
as his vigorous strokes sent the punt along
towards the quay. A delightful sense of
prosperous well-being was upon him. The
cargo he had just sent off was an unusually
large one, and he was feeling, not for the
first time, all the keen exhilaration of having
in the face of opposition started a new enterprise and carried it through by force of his
own pluck and longheadedness.

Fish-buying on this large scale was a
new trade in Rossbrin ; and when Rick came
home from America, and, instead of being
content to invest his savings in land, or in
the manner still more sanctified by custom,
a public-house, set to work to buy barrels
and build stores, the opinion of the place
was that Rick O'Grady's folly was pitiable,
if not impertinent. That was six months

ago, and already the local sages had changed their tune, and pointed to the big stores on the quay as a fitting embodiment of their views on the investment of capital.

Rick had been thrown early on his own resources, and he had hitherto found himself rather more than equal to any emergency that life had offered him. If he was self-confident, he had been justified by success; and though it may be at once admitted that there was nothing at all remarkable about him, except perhaps his good looks, he had a certain stirring, practical quality that always kept him in 'the movement,' whatever it might be. Even in a society so little given to gush as a 'Pork-circle' in Chicago, his push and his clear views about his own interests had wrung from a rival the gratifying if obscure commendation—'There ain't no flies on *him.*' In fact, he was one of those fortunate persons whose brains are so

nicely proportioned to their ambitions that
failure is a word of which they have very
little practical experience.

It has been insinuated that his good looks
were remarkable, but it must be confessed
that they were not of a pre-eminently
classical or intellectual type. His reddish-
brown hair curled a trifle too redundantly on
his broad, low forehead. His nose, though
straight and well shaped, was put on at a
more salient angle than is common in Greek
art. In spite of the thick, dark brows above
them, his sea-blue eyes contrasted rather too
brilliantly with his flamboyant, yellow-red
moustache and fresh-coloured face, and his
head, though small and well set on his
square shoulders, had that thickness above
the ears which, though it has the merit of
betokening force of character, undeniably
spoils its contour.

The punt was soon in the clear, shallow

water alongside the slip, and Rick made her
fast and started up the hill with the air of a
man who has no time to spare. As he
turned the corner by the two large sycamore-
trees he paused to look at his watch before
attacking the steepest pinch of the ascent.

'Half-past four already,' he thought; 'an'
I told her I'd be there by four. Well, afther
all——' He did not finish his thought
intelligibly, but with a half-smile and shrug
of his shoulders went quickly on up the hill,
with his eyes bent downwards towards the
ground, as men are said to look when they
think about the past.

There was only one customer in the bar
of Donovan's hotel—an old woman buying
tobacco, who moved respectfully to one side
to make way for the young man when his
light, strong figure appeared in the doorway. The boy who had brought Donovan's
trap to the door jumped off a cask in the

3

corner, and hurriedly concealing the jew's-harp that had solaced his leisure moments, delivered himself of his message in a slightly amended form.

'Misther Donovan's gone to Scariff, and ye're to step inside in the parlour to wait for him!'

He opened the door at the end of the shop, and Rick passed through it into a dark little passage that smelt like a lodging-house cupboard—a cupboard in which cheese, bread, and mice have been kept. A little light came from three panes of glass in a door at the end of it; Rick knocked, and a voice from inside told him to come in.

Harriet Donovan was sitting in state in her parlour. She was working at a white crochet antimacassar, a companion to those which were hanging cheerlessly over the mahogany backs of the 'suite of dining-room chairs,' which her husband had, on the occasion of his wedding, purchased at a forced sale of one of his numerous creditors. The fire was burning briskly in the small grate, but there was scarcely an ash on 'the polished hearthstone, and the mustiness of the room was sufficient testimony to the fact that it had only been lighted an hour ago. The round oilcloth-covered table was bare of any adornments save a tall vase of artificial flowers, two or three books of gilded devotional exterior, and a tray with glasses and a black bottle of wine on it.

Mrs. Donovan did not rise as her visitor came in ; on the contrary, she leaned back with as good an imitation of fashionable indolence as her high-backed armchair would permit of, and extended a large and passably white hand to her guest.

' I'm very sorry if I kept you waiting, Mrs. Donovan ; I couldn't be here earlier,' Rick said as he took her hand and shook it with the peculiarly hearty ungracefulness of his class. 'The steamer was late startin'.'

He knew as he said it that in making an apology he was placing himself at a disadvantage, but he was one of those fortunate young men who had no objection to placing himself at a disadvantage with a woman, experience having shown him that such a position tended not infrequently to the strengthening of his hand.

Harriet instantly assumed the expected attitude.

'Oh don't mention it, Mr. O'Grady! 'Deed, I scarcely expected you, you were so uncertain about it yesterday ; and I thought it was Mr. Donovan you wanted to see.' As she spoke she was conscious of the accusing presence of the festive preparations on the table. 'Mr. Donovan left a bottle of port-wine out on the chance you'd come,'

she said ; 'won't ye take a glass while ye're
waiting for him ?'

Rick helped himself, and placed a chair
close to hers.

'Ye might know I'd come when I told ye
I would,' he said, with a little judicious
pathos in his voice, 'mightn't ye, now ?'

Mrs. Donovan did not answer, unless the
threefold energy with which she applied
herself to her crochet, and the slow, dark
spread of colour in her pale face, amounted
to a reply. .

Rick finished his glass of wine with a
toss, and wiped his aggressive moustache
with the back of his hand. He had played
the game of making love to Harriet Kelly
many years ago with considerable zest ;
but now that it seemed open to him
to begin it over again on more exciting, if
more perilous lines, he found it had lost its
charm.

'Well, now, what's this that John wants to speak to me about?' he said, changing the conversation to a more practical topic; 'is it League business, or what?'

Whatever Harriet's feelings may have been at this abrupt transition from romance to business, she concealed them very successfully.

'Indeed, I know very little about his business one way or the other,' she answered coldly. 'I believe it's something about that boycotted farm that Mrs. Leonard is after taking. He got a notification about it from the Secretary, in X——, yesterday.'

'It's a good farm,' Rick said meditatively. 'Mahony was a fool to go leave it the way he did!'

'Maybe he's sorry enough now,' said Harriet, with a short laugh; 'and I wouldn't say but Mrs. Leonard 'll be sorry enough too before she's done.'

Rick was silent, as was his manner on receiving information that required to be assorted and compared with what he already possessed. It was characteristic of him that in small matters as well as in great he shielded his opinions in this way, using quite instinctively the best and least offensive method, without an idea of its value. He had lately joined the Rossbrin branch of the Land League, and he knew most of the circumstances in connection with the farm of Drimnahoon. What he did not know was the extent to which the president, John Donovan, trusted his wife. For his part, in spite of, or perhaps in consequence of, his early knowledge of her, he felt inclined to proceed with caution.

'Well, there's no sayin' how things will happen,' he said ; ' but I thought likely the widow 'd have more trouble out of that than she bargained for.' Then, irrelevantly :

'That daughter of hers is a nate little piece.'

Harriet studied the white cotton petals of one of her crocheted roses with a smile that made her lips look thin.

'They - say Dan Hurley, her mother's servant-boy, thinks the same.'

'Is it that white-headed bosthoon that was in chapel with them last Sunday?' said Rick incredulously. 'He's as ugly as if he was bespoke!'

'You've hit it now, said Harriet with another laugh, 'for that's just what he is. Indeed, they're all saying that the widow must be hard set for a son-in-law, if that's the best she can get for her daughter! Well! Maybe she thinks she'd rather be sure, than sorry with ne'er a one at all.'

Rick got up from his chair and began to study the oleograph of Mr. Parnell which occupied the place of honour over the narrow mantelshelf, as if the subject had ceased to interest him.

Harriet felt that she had overshot her mark, and her irritated inner consciousness told her the thought that was passing through Rick's mind with unconscious cynicism—the thought that it was not advisable for him to praise another woman to Mrs. Donovan. She looked up at him with eyes in which something had subdued their usual daring, but her wish to recover her lost ground could find no better utterance than to say :

' However, it's little I know of Ellen Leonard, one way or the other. I dare say it's only foolish talking, after all.' Then, after an instant, tense with the strain of repressing some wild speech or other, she went on : ' I'm sorry you have to be kept here waiting so long for John. It isn't usual with him to be so late. Won't you sit down and take another glass of wine ?'

In his secret soul Rick would have been glad to hear the hotel-keeper's heavy step in the little passage, but he turned from his meditation on the melancholy features of the uncrowned king, and said, with a smile that showed his white teeth to great advantage :

'There's no reason ye should be sorry for me, Mrs. Donovan, so long as I'm not sorry for myself—but for all that, I'm afraid I can't make much more delay.'

She thought him the most beautiful creature she had ever seen, as he stood twisting his orange-coloured moustache and smiling irresolutely at her. He had changed a good deal since the old days, when all Rossbrin knew that he was 'afther Harriet Kelly,' and a sudden fierce hatred filled her for the girl who had allowed him to go to America in disgust with her and all things, because she had thrown him over to marry the richest man in Rossbrin.

' It's like old times, havin' you here,' she said almost timidly—'the times before you went to America. You used to call me " Harriet" then.'

His self-possession did not prevent him from looking rather foolish.

'Oh, that's a long time ago,' he said with some embarrassment. 'There's been many a change since then.'

' I know there has,' Harriet murmured, almost inaudibly ; and then, fixing her dark eyes on his face with such intensity that a fire seemed to kindle in them, ' Rick !' she faltered, 'are ye angry with me still for the way I threated ye ?'

It was the only unpractical point in Rick's character that he could seldom find it in his heart to say anything that would hurt a woman's feelings.

'Angry with ye ! Indeed, ye know I wasn't —at least—of course——' he stammered.

The swing-door between the shop and the passage creaked on its hinges, and the high husky voice that Harriet was learning to hate was heard giving an order to someone outside.

Rick made a snatch at his smart deerstalker cap, and going out into the passage, he greeted Mr. Donovan with a heartiness that was quite unaffected.

CHAPTER IV.

A MOONLIGHT PASTORAL.

THE 'brayching little robber of a red heifer' was absent. True to her promise, Mrs. Leonard had exiled her to the farm of Drimnahoon, where, round James Mahony's empty house, such dainties as flannel-petticoats were not procurable. Perhaps it was in search of some such relish after the monotony of the coarse upland grass that she had wandered from the herd, and drawn upon herself the maledictions of Dan Hurley, who, in the streaming sunrise of a wet October morning, was as usual making the rounds of the farm and counting the stock.

She was certainly not in the field where the other cattle had spent the night. Dan counted them all : nine of them, standing stupidly about in the thick mist, or disconsolately nosing at the soaked grass ; but the tenth, the costliest and best-looking heifer of them all, was nowhere to be seen. Dan crossed the little stream that came oozing down among the rocks and tufts of heather from the height at the back of the farm, and walked along the muddy grass-track in the next field, towards a ragged plantation of larch and laurel. The red heifer was noted as a fencer, and knowledge of her power of 'breaching' a wall made Dan tolerably certain that he would find her in the plantation luxuriously tearing the leaves off the laurels that formed its undergrowth.

But the weak spot in the fence, which she would inevitably have found out, was not

broken through, and a search of the plantation proved fruitless.

' Unless she's above in the cabbage-garden,'
said Dan to himself, ' she's every shtep of the
way back to Scariff this minnit—bad luck to
her !'

He climbed clumsily out over the wall, and
went quickly up the cart-track towards the
cottage, behind which a plot of tilled ground
still showed some heads of cabbages among
the weeds. The house hid the cabbage-
garden from his sight; but as Dan passed
through the gateway into the little yard, he
saw that his search was at an end.

There, tumbled up against the shut door of
the cabin, lay the red heifer, dead, in a pool of
her own blood that had flowed from a dozen
gashes in her sleek skin. Fastened to the
door was a dirty sheet of copybook paper,
with a few crooked lines of writing on it.
Dan walked up to it with a strange trembling

all over him.   The gusts of mist had driven
against the door since long before sunrise,
and had blurred the misshapen letters, so
that he found some difficulty in reading
it.

'Take notis, that this is the way I will
sarve all Land-grabbers.

'CAPTIN MOONLIGHT.'

The usual conventional coffin, barbarously
drawn, put a portentous end to this announce-
ment.   Dan looked fearfully round the yard.
For anything he knew, Captain Moonlight
was waiting to carry out his threat : perhaps
the barrel of his gun was at this minute being
steadied on the sill of one of the little cabin
windows, and was pointing through a broken
pane at him.   The thought kept him fixed
where he was standing, with the veins of his
head throbbing as if a force-pump were at
work there, and his ugly face turning a sort

of blotched gray in colour. After what seemed to him several minutes, he ventured to turn round and look about him. There were the marks of feet in the mud, but no other intimation of human presence was visible. He gathered courage from the stillness to take the paper off the door, and walk away from the house, glancing furtively from side to side as he went.

As soon as he was in the lane he began to run, and, once started, ran faster and faster till he was out in the middle of the big bare field where he had left the rest of the cattle. He stood still there, panting as if he had run a very long distance, and taking the paper out of his pocket, tried to read its contents again ; but he felt himself swaying from side to side, and the words swam before his eyes and faded in a red pulsating mist. A cold sweat broke out all over him, tangible darkness seemed to press in

4 .

upon his spinning brain, then a horror like death.

*　　　*　　　*　　　*　　　*

When he next knew anything he found himself lying on the drenched grass, with stiffened legs drawn up under him, and ice-cold fingers twisted into the coarse tufts of grass. He sat up with difficulty, while recollection of what had happened came slowly back to him. The last time he had had a seizure of this kind had been that day, years ago, when he had watched the work-house van carrying his mother away, and someone—who was it ?—had given him a blow with a stick, and told him he'd have to work now if he didn't want to go to the house too. He had forgotten that blow till now ; it had been blotted out somehow by what had followed it. He struggled on to his feet, still trying to clear his confused mind, when he saw on the ground the paper that he had taken off the door. He picked it up, and as he read the words scrawled on it, the name of the giver of that long-forgotten blow came to him like a hint mysteriously given to help him to the answer of this dark riddle.

In a mind like his, thought is scarcely a coherent process, but resolves itself into a succession of more or less crude emotions. Dan had passed from fright to a kind of slow rage, which was gradually, whether reasonably or no, concentrating itself upon one object, the man who from his childhood had seemed to him the origin of evil as far as he was concerned. If John Donovan had known the oaths and inarticulate threats of hatred and vengeance that were being levelled against him from the cold pastures of the boycotted farm of Drimnahoon, his slumbers in his comfortable feather-bed would have been somewhat disturbed, even though he might have considered that his conscience was technically clear in the matter. To Dan, this attack upon property which he regarded as all but his own seemed the natural culmination of a spite which had shadowed him all his life, and the hatred that had been coiled sluggishly about his heart woke to a quick venomous life.

The Widow Leonard was an early riser, and her household necessarily followed in her vigorous footsteps. At half-past six o'clock, Bridget, the elephantine servant-girl, was giving the pigs their steaming breakfast of black potatoes when Dan came into the yard.

'Ye're home soon, Danny,' she remarked, rubbing the potato flour off her thick arms; 'ye won't get yer brekfish this half-hour.' Then suddenly fixing her eyes on his face, 'Why, thin, what ails ye, at all?' she exclaimed. 'Is it sick y'are?'

Dan's only answer was to walk past her

to the cowhouse, from whose open door came the steady, quiet sound of milking.

Ellen was there, looking, had Dan had the eyes to see it, the realization of all pastoral romance, sitting on a low stool, with her fair head leaned against the rough black side of the cow that she was milking, and with the pale morning light touching her slender figure into emphasis against the dark background of the cowhouse. Her face was of a type more common in the South of Ireland than is generally supposed : a long, almost melancholy oval, with straight brows and grave gray eyes; a beautiful face and a conscientious one, with the smooth half-moon-shaped forehead that generally implies moral rather than intellectual strength.

She had heard Dan's footstep in the yard, and looked round as he came in. He came over and stood beside her silently. Something indefinable about him struck Ellen ;

she stopped her milking, and, looking hard
at him, said, as Bridget had done :

'Why Dan, what ails ye? What brings
ye home so early?'

Dan passed the back of his hand across
his dry lips before he spoke ; then he said
hoarsely :

'The big red heifer's killed above, in
Drimnahoon !'

'Almighty God !' ejaculated Ellen, starting
up ; 'what killed her?'

'They have her near cut to pieces, lyin'
bet up agin Jim Mahony's door,' continued
Dan in the same husky whisper, 'and this
writin' on the door over her,' producing the
paper from his pocket. 'He may call
himself " Captin Moonlight"— the d—d
ruffin !— but as sure as I'm alive this day,
I know well who 'twas !'

'And who was it, Dan ?' gasped
Ellen.

Dan's light eyes peered furtively round the cowhouse, and finally rested on Ellen's white, excited face.

''Twould be no good for me to tell ye,' he said at length, regarding her with an expression in which cunning was curiously blended with fondness. ' But I'll tell ye this much, that 'twould be besht for us to give up Dhrimnahoon.'

' Me mother 'll never give it up!' cried Ellen, the tears that followed on the shock now running down her cheeks. 'Oh, Dan asthore, we're disthroyed! What'll we do at all!'

She seized his hand in her distress, and with her other hand over her swimming eyes, she swayed herself to and fro in a kind of distraction.

There was not much of manhood or courage in Dan, but what there was came uppermost at this crisis.

'Ah, now, don't be cryin',' he said, putting his arm awkwardly round her waist. 'Sure, they'll have to kill me first before I'll let any harm happen to ye !'

His voice shook with the unwonted wave of feeling, and its meaning penetrated through Ellen's fears. She drew herself quickly away from him and let go his hand.

'But mother, Dan !' she said; 'ye didn't tell me mother yet! Let me into the house till I tell her.'

She ran out of the cowhouse before he had time to stop her, and hurried across the yard to the cottage, on the threshold of which her mother was shrilly calling the chickens to their morning meal.

CHAPTER V.

A FEW days after Mrs. Leonard had received
the news of the slaughter of her heifer, Mr.
John Donovan spent a long afternoon at home
in a manner sufficiently agreeable to himself.
He had magnanimously given permission
to his two servants to attend in company a
funeral in the neighbourhood, being aware
that such an attraction as a 'berryin'' would
empty Rossbrin of most of its inhabitants, and
bring business to a standstill for the time.

His accounts kept him pleasantly engaged
during the slow progress of one uneventful
hour, and having finished them, he settled

himself comfortably down to read the *Free-man's Journal*, with his back against a line of mahogany drawers, and his hat tilted over his eyes.   He gave his whole attention to what he was reading, whispering the words to himself with a carefulness that would have been vastly flattering to the editor; but not a foot-fall in the street escaped his practised ear, and the infrequent passer-by was followed for a moment by a sharp glance from under the brim of the seedy pot-hat which was conse-crated to use in the shop.

It is not, perhaps, out of place to note the habit that prevails among tradesmen of Mr. Donovan's class of wearing a hat while administering the affairs of the shop.   It seems to have a threefold purpose : it speaks the master of the house, and his authority, to the poorer customers; it gives, in the taking of it off, a more finished respect for the 'quality,' and its final, and perhaps most interesting, expression is its hint of other and outside affairs, in which the counter and the scales are but an interlude.

In spite of the air of contented languor which apparently pervaded Mr. Donovan on this quiet afternoon, a very close observer might have detected in him some slight touch of expectation, or waiting for some person or event that delayed in coming. Once he had even reached out a big hand and moved a little on one side a decanter of mahogany-coloured sherry that stood in the line of those quick looks out of the window. He had finished the *Freeman*, from the fiery leaders down to the last delusive paragraphic advertisement, when a shadow fell on the paper that was lying on his knees, and he had only just time to take it up, and seemingly absorb himself in its innermost depths, before Ellen Leonard came into the shop.

She hesitated for a minute, looking from one counter to the other, until a rustle from the newspaper made Donovan's presence known to her. The plaid shawl that she wore over her head and shoulders hid most of her face ; it might have been its shadow that lay darkly under her gray eyes, and gave her a look of such weariness and dejection that Mr. Donovan was hard put to it to keep his thick lips from widening into a grin as he noted it ; and noting, too, the whiteness of the cheeks, and the trembling of the small brown hand that rested on the counter, he thought how smartly the admirable discipline of the boycott was being brought to bear upon this daughter of revolt.

'I want a half-pound of tay, Misther Donovan, plaze,' began Ellen, setting a large empty basket down on the floor beside her, and beginning to fumble in the breast of her dress for her purse ; 'and——'

'I'm sold out of tay,' remarked Mr. Donovan curtly.

'Why, then, that's what I'm afther being told at Murphy's and Egan's!' said Ellen, surprise dying into disappointment in her voice; 'I thought there was no fear but I'd get it here.'

Donovan raised the paper and lowered his head to a paragraph at the foot of the page, but said nothing.

'Well, would ye give me a pound of sugar——'

'We don't keep sugar,' Donovan struck in, with his face hidden by the paper.

'Is it not keep sugar!' Ellen said, her fatigue forgotten in her astonishment; 'why, Misther Donovan, it isn't three weeks since I got sugar here!'

'Well, I've none in stock to-day.'

Ellen's face flushed suddenly.

'Well, isn't it a quare thing I can get

nothing I want to-day!' she said, trying to speak lightly. 'But ye have yallow male, whatever.' She pointed to a barrel of Indian corn standing open by the counter. 'I'll be obliged to ye if ye'd give me a stone of that.'

Donovan turned his newspaper inside out very slowly.

'That's all ordhered by different parties,' he said.

He pushed his hat back, and yawned as he looked up and down the columns.

Ellen said no more. She replaced her purse in her bosom, and, taking up her empty basket, she went out into the street. Its familiar outlines and objects were blurred by the tears that fear and mortification forced to her eyes, as she hurried along the uneven pavement, as miserable and as hopeless as James Mahony's most devoted adherent could wish. She understood now the apathy of that usually energetic trader, Mr. John

Donovan, and the amazing scarcity of the necessaries of life in so flourishing a place as Rossbrin. We fear that the qualities of the historical heroine were wanting in Ellen. Political convictions she had none, but her private opinions were, like those of most women of her class, soundly based on expediency, and the first resolution which she came to while speeding along by the high demesne wall was that that bone of contention, the farm of Drimnahoon, should no longer intervene between her mother's household and its daily bread.

She turned in at the gate where Harriet had met her husband, and struck across the broad grass fields to the woods through which lay the short-cut to Scariff. A thin fog was rising with the sunset, and was drawing the horizon into a narrow circle around her. She looked back, as she closed the gate, at the edge of the trees, over the dimmed

grassy stretches, and her heart shrank within
her with a nervousness that was partly
physical and partly superstitious, as she
entered the depth and silence of the woods
that lay between her and home. The trees
stood motionless and mysterious in their
carpet of red leaves, with the pale breath of
the fog creeping about their stems and closing
the vistas between them ; she longed for a
wind to drive the leaves before it, and shake
the ghostly branches, and deaden the loud
fall of her own footsteps. About half-way to
Scariff there came an opening in the wood :
a long narrow glade through which flowed a
river of brown bracken, with big furze bushes
standing in it like dark islands. Ellen walked
steadily on, with the bracken breast-high on
either side of her ; she was less frightened
now, but her nerves still fluttered at every
sound. Suddenly she stood stock-still and
listened.

There was a rustling in the wood at one
side of her, a breaking of branches, and
then a doe leaped out through the bracken,
bucked across the path, and was lost in an
instant in the covert on the other side.
Ellen sprang back with a startled cry, and,
as if in answer, there came a succession of excited squeals from the direction in which the
doe had come, and then a small nondescript
yellow dog darted yelping across the path,
running the hot scent of the doe in an anguish
of excitement, and a passion of belief in its
own powers of overtaking and slaying her.
A dog hunting deer in the much-poached
Trahartha woods was not an unusual circumstance ; of the two, it broke in rather cheer-
fully on the solitude, and Ellen proceeded on
her way with a lighter heart. She had not
gone many steps, however, before her terrors
awoke sevenfold at the dull unmistakable
beat of running footsteps following her up

5

the grassy path.   Then a man's voice shouted to her, angrily she thought, something that she could not understand.   The foolish impulse of flight overcame her, and dropping her big empty market basket, she ran wildly down the path, conscious to agony of the hopeless lengths of lonely wood that lay between her and home.

She ran fast, but her pursuer gained rapidly on her, and it seemed to her that a dreadful laugh, a laugh such as would fitly match the savage motley of a moonlighter, came pantingly after her.   The moment of capture came sooner than she had thought it must come. Something, at once hard and light, came down over her head and stopped her progress, and with a cry like a spent hare, she stumbled forward on to her knees.   Whatever the dreadful engine with which she had been snared was, it was straightway lifted off, and an unmistakably friendly voice exclaimed :

'Bedad! I have ye caught at last! Whoever ye are, ye're a good runner.'

Ellen lifted her fear-stricken face to her captor, and saw Rick O'Grady standing and laughing at her, holding in his hand the thing in which he had encaged her, her own empty basket.

'Oh, Misther O'Grady!' she gasped, 'I didn't think it was you!'

'May I be happy! But it's Ellen Leonard,' responded Rick, still rather breathless, and looking at her with undisguised interest and amusement; 'and what in the name of fortune possessed ye to run that way? Sure, it wasn't you I was hunting at all, but me dog, until I seen ye making tracks, and I was bound to see who ye were, and to tell ye ye'd lost your basket.' He began to laugh. 'I stopped ye pretty handy now, didn't I?'

'I thought,' she panted—'I thought 'twas them that killed our heifer was afther me.'

'And what made ye think such a thing as
that?' said Rick, his blue eyes looking all
the admiration and compassion that he felt.
'I don't think there's any man livin' would
want to hurt ye!'

Ellen gave a cautious glance at his face.
There was no mistaking its friendliness, impossible though it seemed to reconcile it with
the fact that Mr. O'Grady was a prominent
member of the association in whose blackest
books she and her mother were inscribed.
In that instant's study of his face, however,
she made up her mind to trust him, with
a quickness that surprised herself. She
smoothed back the wisps of yellow hair that
had straggled over her forehead, and with a
sidelong look from under her thick eye-
lashes :

'If I knew it was you, I wouldn't have
been frightened,' she said ; 'but since ever I
seen that paper they put up over the heifer

they killed in Dhrimnahoon, I'd be afraid of
everyone I meet.'

She had begun to walk on towards Scariff,
and Rick, still carrying her basket, strolled
along beside her.

' I wouldn't mind the half them blackguards
would threaten ; they haven't the grit to do
more than kill a cow,' Rick answered, with
the contempt for his fellow-countrymen which
the Irishman usually imports from America.

' Anyone that would slaughther an innocent
baste for spite would think little to kill the
likes of me or me mother.' She hesitated,
then with an anxious look up at his handsome face : ' I undherstand we're to be boycotted altogether now,' she said timidly.

Rick cleared his throat uncomfortably.

' The League had no more to say to the
heifer being killed than you had yourself ;
that was no part of the boycotting.'

Ellen saw her advantage.

'I brought in that basket,' she said, ' the way I do every week, to get it filled with the little things we'd want in the house ; but there was ne'er a one in Rossbrin, Misther Donovan himself, nor one of them, would sell me a grain of tay—no, nor sugar, nor male nayther ; and 'tis the same thing to be starved as killed whatever !'

Rick's eyes fell mechanically on the basket on his arm. It gave admirable point to her story, but he said nothing. The little yellow dog had some time before returned, with the guiltiest of consciences, from its pursuit of the doe, and having trotted cautiously in the rear for some time, now gathered courage to sneak past its master, with tail sunk, and a wary eye fixed on his face. To its surprise, it received no rebuke. Rick was looking straight on ahead of him into the foggy gloom of the wood, his mind struggling with a new view of a social problem that he thought he had mastered in every aspect. He had forgotten the difficulties that attend on the personal application of an abstract theory.

'Well,' he said at length, 'I think your mother had best give up that farm as quick as she can. She'll get no good of going agen the League.'

'I know that well,' Ellen answered with pathetic conviction; 'but ye might as well be talking to them that's dead as to me mother. I think if she seen every cow she has, and me with them, killed forninst her two èyes, 'twould be the same story with her—she'd howld on to Dhrimnahoon.'

Her voice broke a little as she ended, and she put out her hand and let it fall to her side with a gesture of utter dejection. They had walked fast, and were now almost at the farther verge of the wood, and they could hear in front of them the Rowrie River fight-

ing its way downwards between high rocky
banks to the sea. Just where the path
emerged from the wood stood the low, roof-
less ruin of a mill, a desolate place, with its
gray stones held together by the thick ropes
of ivy that had knotted themselves round it.
The timbers of the wheel had long ago rotted
away from the rusty iron axle that projected
from the gable-end above the river ; the mill-
stones lay on the earthen floor inside, half
hidden by dead leaves, and the foot-bridge
that had been the mill's connecting-link with
the Scariff side of the river was now no more
than a couple of long fir-trees, laid across the
narrow gorge, with slimy, decaying logs
nailed side by side upon them to make a
footway, and a thin wooden rail on one side,
intended to impart security, but far more
calculated to betray any trust rashly placed
in it.

At the bridge Ellen turned.

' Thank you for carryin' the basket,' she said, putting out her hand for it.

Rick could see her face clearly in the comparative lightness outside the wood, and could note the plaintive droop of lips whose perfectness he only dimly felt, and the traces of tears under the soft gray eyes. He took her hand in his.

' Well, good-bye !' he said constrainedly ; ' here's your basket. I'm sorry I gave ye such a fright in the wood.' He turned away at once.

Ellen went across the bridge and up the lane that led from it to her mother's house, feeling that her little flicker of hope had been pitilessly put out.

CHAPTER VI.

APPLIED PRINCIPLES.

A MINUTE or so after Ellen had parted from
Rick O'Grady a tragedy of a small and
common kind was enacted within fifty yards
of the bridge. Between two ash-trees,
whose arching roots formed the openings of
an intricate series of rabbit burrows, ran the
tiny track worn by the rabbits in their soft-
footed goings to and fro, and here, half
hidden by dead leaves, had lain since mid-
day an unsuspected and venomous-looking
trap. In the twilight feeding hour its mission
was fulfilled, and following on the harsh
snap of its iron teeth, the still gray air

was torn by the screams of the miserable little victim.

The rabbit's pangs were short. A man who had a moment before started up, as if from a hiding-place, in a thicket of furze, near the bridge, and was standing looking at Ellen Leonard's disappearing figure, turned and came along towards the sound, swinging by its heels a dead rabbit that he held in his left hand. The brutal act of mercy to the living one was quickly accomplished, and tying both their hind-legs together, Dan Hurley went on along the river bank with his spoil. He visited two or three more traps with varying success, and finally, having reached the bounds of the widow's farm, he struck across the fields for the house.

The small soul that dwelt in his ungainly body was seething with jealous fright and perplexity as he thought of the parting on the bridge that he had just seen. What

right had Ellen to walk alone through the
woods with that — very ugly adjectives
rose in Dan's mind as he thought of Rick
O'Grady and his smart clothes.   And he,
high up in the League, what call had he to
be trying to spy on them he was boycotting?
It was making a fool of Ellen he was, and
so he, Dan, would tell her, and if she didn't
choose to mind him, it'd be the worse for
them that came between him and her.

It was quite dark when he got to the
cottage, and through the open half of the
door he saw Mrs. Leonard and Ellen at
their tea.   He came in without speaking,
and, flinging down the rabbits on the dresser,
dragged a stool up to the table and sat down.
Mrs. Leonard poured him out a cup of tea
from the broken-nosed pot, and pushed it
towards him, saying:

'There's yer tay!'

After which she fell again into a silence

which from its extreme unusualness was clearly an intentional signal of wrath.

The meal was not an elaborate one : on the bare boards of the table was set the tea equipage, consisting of the teapot, once brown, now burnt black from long stewings in the hot ashes, a cracked white and blue bowl full of soft sugar, a jug of milk, and a large cake of home-made soda bread. From this last Ellen cut an immense triangle and handed it silently to Dan. He looked about for the usual coarse loaf of baker's bread, which the Irish peasant has so frequently the bad taste to prefer to his own admirable griddle-baked bread.

'Where's the loaf-bread?' he asked Ellen in an undertone.

His voice was all that was needed to loosen the impending avalanche.

'Ha thin! Bread indeed!' began Mrs. Leonard with a wholly inexpressible snort;

' 'tis little baker's bread ye'll be gettin' from
this out! Ye'll have to contint yerself with
pittaties now—for so grand as ye are, Dan
Hurley!'

Dan paused in the act of pulling the dough
out of his soda bread with his fingers.

' Why not ?' he demanded laconically.

' Why not ?' repeated the widow, her voice
rising to the pitch necessary for declamation.
' Why not ? Ask Ellen, that has walked the
town of Rossbrin through and fro this day,
askin' for tay and sugar, and wouldn't be
given as much as would blind yer eye! An'
me, as good a Land Layguer as any one of
them ; let alone John Donovan that has yer
mother's farm this minnit ! Aha ! well I
know why I'm boycotted—he have his eye
cocked on Dhrimnahoon for himself !'

' An' if he have,' said Ellen in the wearied
voice of a person who adds one more to a
series of disregarded arguments, ' 'tis as

good for us to give it to him. Shure the
world knows that whatever thing he'll want,
he'll never stop nor stay till he have it.'

Mrs. Leonard slopped the remains of her
cup of tea into her saucer with a defiant
flourish.

' May this be the last dhrop of tay I put
into me mouth if I ever give up Dhrimnahoon to him or the likes of him !'

She took a sounding gulp from her saucer,
and dramatically flung the dregs into the hot
turf ashes on the hearth, with such a suddenness that the musing cat retreated to the
fastnesses beneath the dresser with a tail
thickened with alarm and resentment.

Ellen leaned her head back against the
discoloured whitewashed wall behind her
and said no more. Dan stolidly went on
with his supper. In his heart he thought
Mrs. Leonard a fool even to think of pitting
herself against the League, but he was afraid

to tell her so—afraid to say or do anything
that might lower him in her good graces.
He looked at Ellen furtively once or twice;
the dull, jealous rage and distrust of an hour
ago was still hot in him, and he longed to put
some question that would force her to explain her walk through the wood with Rick
O'Grady. Perhaps, in the silence, the single
strenuous direction of his thought insensibly
made a way for itself into the minds of the
others.

'What's this ye were tellin' me about
Rick O'Grady?' resumed the widow, who
had taken up her knitting and was working
at it with incredible speed. 'Me head's that
moidhered that I dunno the half ye were
sayin'.'

'He said what I'm saying to ye all
through,' responded Ellen, still leaning her
pretty head against the wall, as if she were
too tired, mentally and bodily, to move.

'He said we should give up the farm ; he was friendly enough, but that was the only word he had for me !'

'That's the fine frinnship !' hooted Mrs. Leonard ; 'the divil thank him for his frinnship ! I suppose it's all in the way of frinnship that him and the rest of them are playin' on us this way ! B'leeve me, if 'twas in Rossbrin ye were walkin' in place of the back of the woods, ye'd not find him so frindly !'

At this point there broke in on her discourse a prolonged and fretful bleating of a calf in one of the sheds outside.

' 'What ails the calf this way ?' she demanded of Dan. 'Didn't Jerry feed him ?'

'I didn't see Jerry since dinner,' Dan answered in his loud grumbling voice.

'He'd betther mind out for himself before I ketch him, lavin' his work this way !' said Mrs. Leonard wrathfully ; 'when well he

6

knows that that big flahool of a Bridget went
from me yistherday—may the divil roast her !
and there's her work to be done, let alone
his own.'

'He towld me this morning his father
got ordhers he wouldn't be let work here
any more,' said Dan, 'and I dunno did
he go home then or no.'

The widow regarded him speechlessly,
as Job might have stared at the last of the
messengers of evil.

'That'll do,' she said at last with a kind
of difficulty ; 'that'll do. When me own
mother's sisther's son would forbid his child
to work for me, I'll say no more.' Then
with a sudden flash : 'Can't ye go out
yerself, ye gommoch, and give a bit to the
crayture that's roarin' for it ? I suppose
you'll be lavin' me next ? But there's no
fear I'll hindher ye. If there wasn't a one
left in this house only meself and the Lord

Almighty I'd stay in it if the town of Ross-brin came to put me out!'

Instead of replying, Dan took up a battered tin can that stood in the corner and went out.

The flame of the paraffin-lamp that hung against the wall gave a smoky leap with the opening and shutting of the door. It roused Ellen as her mother's voice had failed to do, and, getting up, she shut the door, and began to tidy up the house. She got through the various small household duties mechanically, but with a neatness that was second nature to her; and having finally carried in a heavy apronful of turf from the big rick in the yard, she made up the fire, propping the long brick-like sods on their ends, with a skill that embodied more scientific principles of firemaking than she was aware of. The kindly blaze began at once to make its way through the brown pile and the soft

6—2

blue smoke, and putting a stool in the
chimney corner, Ellen sat down with her
elbows propped on her knees and her tired
head resting in her hands. Her fingers
were pressed against her closed eyelids, as
if to enforce on herself some activity of mind,
to help her to think hard and quickly of
some plan or other by which to work on the
feelings of the League; and perhaps, most
of all, to shut out the remembrance of its
president, with his fat face half buried in his
newspaper, and his husky voice that in three
commonplace sentences had explained to her
her position.

Her mother's needles clicked on like
machinery; they were the only things
moving in the quiet house, except for an
occasional stir and sleepy croak from the
hens roosting on a beam at the other end
of the room. In the silence Ellen began
to realize almost wildly the horrors that

might be ahead, with no one to look to for help but Dan—she lifted her head from her hands at that thought with a shudder; was she prepared to pay the price that she intuitively knew Dan would be likely to set on his loyalty ?

The widow moved round quickly when Ellen looked up, as if to bring her knitting under the light ; but quick though she was, Ellen saw her put her apron to her eyes for an instant. Her heart almost stood still at the sight. She had never before known her mother cry, and she believed that she now saw the despair of the strong spirit she had always leaned on. She started up, intending to kneel down before her mother in a last entreaty, when a step outside the door made her stop short. It was not Dan's hobnailed tread ; the blood rushed to her face as she thought of what it might betoken. The widow heard it too, and, getting up, tramped with determination to the door.

'Who's there ?' she called out, in a voice whose very ferocity bespoke an inward alarm.

'A friend,' replied a voice with a slight Yankee twang that seemed familiar to Ellen's straining ears.

'And what may yer name be ?' asked Mrs. Leonard, still in tones of thunder.

'I think if ye'll open the door ye'll not have occasion to ask me that,' was the reply, with a good-humoured laugh.

'It's all right, mother !' whispered Ellen, almost laughing, too, in her relief; 'it's Misther O'Grady.'

She opened the door, and they saw Rick standing outside in the moonlit fog, with the collar of his overcoat turned up round his face, and holding in his hand a large box or parcel of some kind.

' I was sorry to hear the shops in Rossbrin couldn't oblige ye to-day with what ye wanted,' he said, looking hard at Ellen, ' and so, as I happened to have got a box of groceries over in the fish - steamer, I thought that maybe some of them might come handy to ye.'

As he spoke he wondered whether he looked like the lie he was telling, but to Ellen he seemed little short of a messenger from heavenly places.

CHAPTER VII.

THE WAY OF TRANSGRESSORS.

THE Rossbrin Roman Catholic chapel stood about half a mile out of the town at the foot of a high rocky hill—a long plain whitewashed building, distinguished only from the secular barn by its abnormal size, and by a small stone arch on the eastern end of the roof, with a cross on the top of it. The arch had been destined to hold the bell, but experience having shown that the half of the parish that lay on the northward side of the hill could scarcely catch so much as a tinkle of the most strenuous summons to prayer, an ingenious change had been made, and the bell now swung in a wooden cage on the top of the hill itself, to the spiritual welfare of those ultramontane parishioners who did not possess a clock, and the indignation of the old sexton, whose duty it was to climb up the hill and ring it.

November the first, All Saints' Day, is, as everyone knows, a notable feast in the Church of Rome, and twice on that morning the shrill voice of the bell had called from its furze-covered steeple to all the parish of Rossbrin. The early Mass had been numerously attended, but it was at eleven o'clock that the congregation mustered in its greatest strength, and at the close of the long service the green chapel-yard was scarcely large enough for the crowd that streamed from the chapel doors, bringing with it a tainted whiff of hot air and frieze coats, and a babel of deferred gossip in English and Irish. The day was brilliantly fine, and the people were in no hurry to disperse, but formed themselves by a process of natural selection into groups, and gave themselves up to the charms of unrestrained conversation.

Almost the last persons to leave the chapel were two women, who hesitated for a moment in the porch, before stepping down among their neighbours. Instantly there was a slight but noticeable movement among the crowd : there was no diminution in the gabble of talk, but the groups about the central path contracted so that it was left clear, and as the two women passed down to the gate, it would have been only possible for them to recognise their female acquaintances by the difference of colour or of texture in the long-hooded backs of their cloaks. The men were, for the most part, clustered about the gate, and they also drew aside to let the two outcasts from society pass; but, unlike their womenkind, they took little trouble to feign unconsciousness of their presence, some even staring broadly at the Widow Leonard's hot, defiant face in its setting of snowy capfrill, and loud facetious whispers following her and Ellen on their way, told them that their neighbours found much enjoyment in their discomfiture.

A fashionable party was walking in front of them down the lane to the main road, Mrs. Donovan's strong voice and noisy laugh rising above the others as she turned from time to time to fling a remark to Rick O'Grady, who was walking just behind the rest. Ellen put a hand on her mother's cloak.

'Let them out on the road before us,' she whispered.

Rick's visit to the farm of two nights ago

might, for all she knew, have been an isolated
whim of kindness, and for his sake as well as
her own, she did not dare put him to the
test of a public recognition.   But Mrs.
Leonard was devoid of all such refinements
of feeling.   She twitched her cloak from
Ellen's hand and at once quickened her pace,
with the result that the pair drew level with
Rick just at the moment when Harriet, with a
look that was meant for him alone, turned and
asked him if he was coming home with them.
He did not even hear her; he had turned
with smiling politeness to wish the Leonards
good-morning; he was even—Harriet could
scarcely believe her eyes, but it was true
—taking off his hat with a Transatlantic
alertness to those whom Rossbrin and the
League had decided to ignore, and who were
at the best of times nothing but 'common
countrywomen.'

Ellen and her mother passed quickly by,

the former flushed to a lovely colour by a
mark of respect that she had never received
before, and least of all expected now. At
the corner of the lane they took the turn
opposite to that of the Rossbrin contingent,
and were soon out of sight.

' Upon me word !' observed - Miss Vickery,
the Rossbrin modiste, who, walking in front
with Mr. Donovan, had not noticed Rick's
action, ' there's some is very brazen ! I think,
Mr. Donovan, when parties refuses to take the
advice of friends, 'twould be as well for them
to stay at home and not *ex*pose their igner-
ance, and I may say impairtinence, this
way.'

Miss Katty Vickery thrust her little person forward inside her black beaded dolman
and drew down the corners of her mouth with
a righteous spasm of indignation.

' If I'm not greatly mistaken,' replied Mr.
Donovan, who was walking consequen-

tially along in the middle of the road,
much morally upheld by the consciousness of a clean 'dicky' shirt-front and a pair
of creaking boots, 'them parties 'll not come
to chapel agin till they have their minds
med up to leshen to their friends' advice,
supposin' that in the meantime they gets no
encouragements from them that has a right
to know better than to be patteronizin' them.'

Mr. Donovan spoke very loud, and looked
hard at Miss Vickery, exhibiting a profile of
great severity to those behind him. Clearly,
that Transatlantic flourish of Rick's hat had
not escaped his notice.

'Indeed, they'll get no encouragements
from me,' said Miss Vickery, with rancorous
energy. ''Tis no trouble to me to do without Mrs. Leonard's custom. If 'twas only
the makin's of an apron she was buyin', she'd
be huckstherin' and bargin' there till midnight, if I'd let her.'

Harriet struck into the conversation with a shrill laugh.

'Well, Miss Vickery, whatever trouble Mrs. Leonard gave you, it's little the daughter ever troubled your dressmaking, nor hat-making neither! It's surprisin' the way them counthry girls will be content to go about with nothing only an old shawl wisped over their heads.'

Mr. Ryan, the postmaster, was walking between her and Rick, and she turned to him for assent, thereby affording him a fuller view of the stupendous stack of grass-green ribbons that adorned her black hat. Mr. Ryan, an elderly widower, to whom the question had never before presented itself, looked straight in front of him with an expression of respectful and sympathetic imbecility, and murmured:

'Quite so, ma'am—quite so.'

Harriet's eyes passed on from him to Rick,

the smile dying out that had masked the anger in their depths. He was walking on the grass by the side of the road, with his hands in his pockets and his eyes cast down. He was unaware of Harriet's glance ; he was seeing, through the haze of seven years, a black-haired girl leaning over the gunwale of a punt, to look at the reflection of a red plaid shawl that he had bought for her and tied about her head. He raised his eyes and saw the same face, the youth and softness gone out of it, and with a look in it that warned him he was in another era of his life, and one in which it behoved him to walk with caution.

CHAPTER VIII.

THE YELLOW PUNT.

IT was the Sunday next after the Feast of All Saints. The Donovan Sabbath dinner had passed through its first and second stages of boiled pork and greens, and a mound of sodden pancakes, to its finale of hot whisky and water, and clouds of strong tobacco. Mr. Donovan leaned back in his chair, with the three lower buttons of his waistcoat un-fastened, and that expression of having done a commendable thing which most men wear when they have made a large and satisfactory meal. He puffed sententiously at his pipe, and took slow sips of his punch, as if at peace

7

with himself and all the world, while from time
to time he looked from beneath the folds of his
heavy eyelids at the handsome discontented
face of his wife, who was sitting at the other
side of the fireplace, affecting to read the
local weekly paper.

Since the last appearance of Joanna with
the kettle neither had spoken.   Donovan
was not a man much given to words, and,
moreover, he was so thoroughly occupied with
his own slowly-moving thoughts that he did
not notice the silence.   His occasional glances
at his wife were evidently the outcome of
what was going on in his mind ; they were
cautious and speculative, and were, in fact, a
measurement of her outward seeming against
a certain theory that had lately occurred to
him.

At length, after some preliminary rubbing
of his hairy chin and throat with his hand, he
seemed to make up his mind to a line of

action. There is, perhaps, no creature so
Machiavellian in the subtleties of conversation
as an Irishman of John Donovan's type; but
either the lubricating influence of the whisky
and water, or the unexpected circumstance
that in his own unspiritual way he loved his
wife, had the effect of making him approach
the subject more directly than he could have
wished.

'That was a tremenjous take of fish they
had last night,' he began, looking meditatively into the fire; 'I'm told they were up
all night salting it on the pier.'

'Were they?'

Harriet dropped out the monosyllables
as if the effort of opening her mouth was too
much for her.

'It's a fine thrade,' Donovan continued;
'there's no sayin' the money O'Grady has
med out of it this season.'

No answer from Harriet.

7—2

'But 'tis an oncertain thrade all the same, and no one knows that betther than himself.' He cleared his throat, and took a sip of whisky and water. 'He was sayin' to me this two or three days ago that when he had a bit more money put together, he'd be for goin' back to the States. "I have enough of this owld counthry," says he, "and as for Rossbrin, I'd be dead if I was livin' in it."' John Donovan's eye travelled warily across the fireplace in the wake of this ingenious falsehood to observe its effect upon his wife.

'That's strange,' said Harriet in tones of ice, though not all her self-control could stay the colour from tingeing her cheek. 'It was only yesterday evening he told me he was thinking he'd build new stores down there on the quay.'

'Where did ye see him yestherday evenin'?' said Donovan quickly, his brain seeming to leap with a new suspicion. 'Was that you that I seen in the punt with him?'

'I was waitin' for the ferry-boat to go across the water to see my aunt,' replied Harriet; 'and as Mr. O'Grady was going out to the steamer, he offered to put me across first.'

She felt her position to be unassailable, and Donovan recognised that direct attack would be useless. He mixed himself his second tumbler of punch, of an even more tawny complexion than its predecessor, and addressed himself again to the conversation on new lines.

'O'Grady's a smart young man at his business,' he began reflectively; 'but if he wants to have any respect from the people of this place, he'll have to mind himself. I don't considher his principles is very sound. There was plenty remarked his conduct to them Leonards comin' out of chapel on the

Holyday last week, and plenty spoke to me
about it, what's more.'

Harriet laughed contemptuously.

' It's because there isn't one here that has
as much knowledge or manners as would
make them take off their hat to a friend, that
they think such great things of it.'

Undue courtesies of this kind were not
among Mr. Donovan's weaknesses, and he
answered to the whip with a readiness that
showed it had cut him.

'I'm not disputin' that he's a d——d fine
gentleman,' he said, with an ugly sneer ; ' but
as fine as he is, he wouldn't be so well
pleased if he heard what was said to me
th'other night.'

' Little he cares what anyone in this place
says about him!' flashed out Harriet. forgetting
prudence in a sudden whirl of repulsion for
the leering, malevolent face opposite to her.

' Well, by what I could undherstand,' replied

Donovan, gaining calm as she lost it, 'they say he has a great wish to please Ellen Leonard. Of course, there's no sayin' if it's thrue or no,' he went on, with a tone in his husky voice that Harriet knew boded evil ; 'for the matther of that, he was never the boy to be thrustin' to one sweetheart ; but, plaze God, it won't be much longer before I'll have that matther sifted, and then it'll be seen what the League 'll have to say to him.'

Harriet rose to her feet with such a fire burning in her heart as she had never known before. The hidden raw that she scarcely owned to in her own thought had been touched by her husband's coarse hand, and the torture was almost unendurable. She felt she could kill him as she looked down on him, stretched out in sodden comfort before the fire, with an egotistical smile on his heavy face, and his fat hand caressing his tumbler of whisky and water. She felt she

must turn upon him, and tell him how she
loathed and despised him, and how that
some day, maybe, she'd prove to him that
was a lie about Ellen Leonard, in a way that
wouldn't please him.   Her strong white
hands clenched and unclenched with a fever-
ish desire for action ; she turned to leave
the room, pushing her chair back so
roughly that it tilted over and fell on its back
on the floor.

Donovan laughed, the comfortable laugh
induced by a second tumbler of punch.

'Don't ye know that's a sign ye won't be
married this year?' he said jocosely ; 'any way,
I won't give ye a shance if I can help it.
Where are ye goin' ?' he continued, as Harriet
went quickly to the door. 'Come on, me gerrl,
and give me a kiss.'   He lolled his head backwards over his chair towards where he believed she was, but was only in time to see
her open the door and go out.

He heard her go upstairs, and then her quick footstep sounded in the room overhead. He chuckled.

'She's in the divil of a temper now,' he said softly; 'but she's a fine gerrl, whatever.'

He yawned, and gave the fire a kick with the heel of his boot, and when, a minute or two later, Harriet came downstairs with her hat and brown ulster on, she heard his snores vibrating through the wooden partition of the passage.

She let herself out by the side-door, and after a moment's hesitation she turned down the hill. The usual Sunday loungers were hanging about the corner where the two brother sycamores stood in their huge stone and mortar flower-pot in the middle of the street, and one or two of the poorer men touched their hats to Mr. Donovan's wife. Harriet was scarcely popular enough to make the others stretch a point in her

favour, and they, for the most part, averted
their eyes as she passed to avoid the difficulty
of deciding as to the form of salutation, waiting till she had gone by to expend on her the
cynical criticism of complete idleness.

The steep fall of the hill was ended by the
gate of the lower entrance into the Trahartha
woods, and Harriet turned in there instead of
passing on to the pier. A cold, gusty shower
came driving up the harbour, and she hurried
along the path by the water's edge to gain
the shelter of the trees. She could see
through the quick, stinging rain the boats
lying moored in Sunday quietness, and she
noticed at once the absence of Rick
O'Grady's yellow punt from its accustomed
place. In the frame of mind in which she
then was, it was only to be expected that she
should at once picture to herself the yellow
punt hauled up by the little landing-place
in Scariff Bay, while its owner—a wave

of incredulous scorn swept the thought away.

Like many another woman who has caught too late at a love once patiently proffered, she could not believe that her opportunity was lost for ever, and that she was grasping at a thing that was dead. She had been well content to marry the rich hotel-keeper, and had been used to think with a mild, sentimental complacency of Rick, eating his heart out for her in America. The position had become habitual; when Rick O'Grady came back after seven years, she looked forward to his return as sure to infuse a certain delicate element of romance into a life that had become monotonous, with talks of old times, and veiled but sufficient hints of an unchanged devotion. Rick came home friendly, self-sufficing, well-to-do, and so obviously absorbed in the present and its prospects that the only sign of his not having quite forgotten the past was the noticeable care he took not to allude to it.

It was nearly four months since the first doubt of Rick's 'unchanged devotion' had crossed her mind; but though she knew that during that busy time he had scarcely spoken to any other woman, doubt had turned to anxiety, and anxiety to pique, and so on through the vexed, familiar ways of growing passion, till the hidden fight in her strong nature became so unendurable that, on this stormy afternoon of wild white gleams of sunlight and sudden angry dashes of rain, a venomous word had had strength to drive her out to wander in the woods with one unreasoning longing for her guide, to find out for herself if it were true, if it *could* be true, this that her husband had said, that Rick had forgotten her and was courting Ellen Leonard.

The wind followed her boisterously along the narrow path, and sent the wet red leaves whirling round her feet. The fir-trees that leaned over to the sea on her right swung in the gusts and slashed the water with their flat arms, and even at this sheltered part of the estuary, the cold green current of the out-going tide was rough with little white-tipped waves. Harriet kept on her way along the path by the water's edge with a haste that took no heed of the weather. There was only one more point between her and the lake-like widening of the creek into Scariff Bay, and she now noticed that there would not be water enough even for the yellow punt to get up to the landing-place near the mouth of the Rowrie River. She walked on more slowly, the hope that Rick had not gone to Scariff, after all, struggling with the disappointment of not meeting him, when through an opening in the trees on the seaward side of the path a gleam of yellow caught her eye. She climbed cautiously down the steep bank and looked over the low cliff; there, hauled up on a little strand, was the punt.

Then he *had* gone to Scariff! Harriet struggled up to the path again, and almost ran down the rocky slope to a spot farther on where a series of rough steps led from the path to the sea-level, resolved that, no matter what came of it, she would see him now. She had scarcely arrived at them when a footstep in the wood ahead of her made her heart stand still, and by what seemed to her an incredible coincidence, Rick came along between the trees towards her.

He had seen her before she had seen him, and this slight advantage had given him time to determine the exact details of what he was going to say, so that his manner as he came forward to meet her had in it just the right amount of pleased surprise.

'Hello! Mrs. Donovan, that's bad weather for ye to be out walking! Where are ye going at all ?'

For the life of her Harriet could not have repressed the question with which she answered his.

'And where have *you* been to, Mr. O'Grady ?'

Her voice was set to the right pitch of arch suggestion, but a little failing. gasp on the last word told that the answer would be a momentous one to her.

'Oh, is it me ?' said Rick. ' If ye'll promise not to tell Tom Kearney, or to make game of me for being at me old poaching ways, I'll tell ye. I was up at an otter-trap I fixed above by the waterfall, and I might have saved meself the journey, for the divil an otter was there since I set it last night.'

He looked at her with the inscrutable bright smile that charmed her against her

will, and made her face relax into a softened
self-consciousness, and he felt that his
half-truth had successfully shielded another
episode of the afternoon.

'-I don't want to make game of you,' she
said, dropping her eyes, and restlessly
working the moss off a rock at her feet with
the point of her umbrella. Then, as if
suspicion had again plucked at her sleeve,
'it's a deal more likely you're making game
of me. I suppose it was trapping otters
kept you from chapel this morning.'

Rick laughed easily.

' If I'd known you were looking out for me,
you bet I'd have gone; but I got out of the
way of chapel-going when I was across the
water. Look here now,' he went on;
'wouldn't it be as good for ye to let me put
ye home in the punt? 'Twouldn't be the
first time I done that much for ye !'

It was not a highly creditable move on

Rick's part, but it must be remembered that his training had not been of a kind to develop his moral sense, and the danger of discovery had been sharp. There was, from his point of view, much to be gained in his being seen by the world of Rossbrin rowing home the wife of the President of the Land League; and as for her, it was a stroke of luck that had given him this chance of putting himself right with her : in the last few minutes he had become intensely aware that there is no such sharpener of a woman's wits as jealousy.

Harriet was silent for a moment after Rick had spoken ; she was beating about for words in which should escape no fragment of the delight that filled her like a glow.

' It's as good a way of getting home as another. I'll come if you like, Rick.'

She could not help looking up at him as

8

she finished, her brilliant eyes losing their hardness, and her sallow face transfigured by the magic of sudden colour.

'Well, I guess I do like it' answered Rick, going down the steps, and holding out his hand to help her. She stepped into the punt without a word, and he pushed it out from the shore.

CHAPTER IX.

REJECTED.

THE fair of Cloonmore had been a large one. All day long the hoarse hum of voices ascended from the crowded market-place, forming, like the drone of a bagpipe, a monotonous accompaniment to the furious cadenzas of the pigs and the blatant lamentations of the sheep and cattle.

There had been a light soft rain since early morning, and the steam and smell of wet frieze rose opulently upon the heavy air, while buyers and sellers stood contentedly about in mud of a depth and blackness only procurable at an Irish fair, and wrangled

8—2

and lied with a leisurely indifference to
circumstances. The buying had been brisk,
and the prices good, and by half-past three
the streets were emptying fast, the dealers
having taken their purchases away by train,
and the fortunate sellers being, for the most
part, congregated in the innumerable public-
houses of the town.   There had been a good
show of cattle, fat and well-favoured, and very
few remained unsold towards the close of the
day, and it was therefore all the more surprising that at two o'clock Dan Hurley
might have been seen driving out of the
town the beasts he had driven into it soon
after daybreak.

The widow had taken warning by the
slaughter of the red heifer, and since the out-
rage the remaining nine had been safely
stalled down at Scariff every night.   There
had been no animals in the country to touch
them in size and condition ; Mrs. Leonard's

parting injunction to Dan had been to 'keep a shtiff lip' about their price, and she had gone back into her house with a complacent certainty that that night the rents of Scariff and Drimnahoon would be safe in her pocket.

Dan had thought little of the fact that Mr. John Donovan had driven past him into Cloonmore that morning, and had pervaded the fair in his usual slow, occupied manner : the gombeen man was wont to hold quiet dealings with a very large variety of people on occasions of this kind. But as the day wore on, and the heifers were not only not bid for, but actually avoided, he began to realize what was the drift of the confidences that Mr. Donovan was exchanging with his numerous friends and acquaintances.

He stood there with his cattle, a dejected group in the damp and dirt of the fair ; the people shouldering past him as if he did not

exist, while each moment his hatred for his
enemy ran stronger and hotter in his veins.
He longed to escape from this hateful public
pillory of defeat, but he could not face the
humiliation of the moment when the people
would part to make a way for the excom-
municated to sneak out from among them
in full and final acknowledgment of failure.
It was not till the movement for the afternoon train had begun that he started for
home, and at four o'clock he was still very
far from the end of his ten mile journey.
The November evening had fallen gloomy
and thick, and the wet gray walls marked out
the road in front of him in dreary perspective.
The cattle plodded patiently along, and Dan
followed in their rear, turning over in his
narrow mind ceaseless schemes for avenging
him of his enemy, with an inventive perti-
nacity that half surprised himself. He knew
by intuition that the League had little to say

to this matter; he saw in it only the private spite of one man, and, as he walked, there still kept ringing in his ears the curses screamed by his dying mother when the hospital van came to take her from the cabin that was no longer hers to the workhouse infirmary.

'Hoy!' a loud voice shouted behind him, 'dhrive them bastes a-one side'

Dan picked up a stone and flung it with practised aim at the leading heifer, turning her into the ditch, as Mr. Donovan's old mare and trap rattled up alongside of him. 'Is that you, Dan?' called out Donovan; 'I suppose ye couldn't get yer price for the heifers?'

Dan made no answer.

'Maybe the feeding in Dhrimnahoon didn't sarve them,' continued Mr. Donovan with a hoarse laugh, looking back over his shoulder as he whipped up his mare and jolted on in front of Dan and his cortége.

It was a long tramp home to Scariff, but
Dan was scarcely aware of stony hill or
muddy hollow, or the tedious lengths of flat
bog road ; the heat and confusion of rage in
his head seemed to drive him along without
his own volition ; long as the road was, it
was not long enough for the perfecting of
certain schemes in which Mr. John Donovan
and Rick O'Grady took involuntarily leading
parts.

The Scariff farmyard, never at the best of
times a place to be passed through dryshod,
was deep in mire and slush, and the hoofs of
the tired cattle made little sound as they
passed through it, and found their own way
to the shed from which they had been driven
in the early morning. Dan fastened the door
on them, and stood irresolutely looking at the
lighted window of the cottage, wondering
what Mrs. Leonard would say to the news
he had to tell her, and how Ellen would like

it—Ellen, that had said the night that Rick O'Grady brought them the present of the tea, that no harm would happen them, now that they had the likes of him. for a friend. Maybe she'd change her tune now.

He had taken a step towards the house when the sound of voices in the bohireen outside the yard arrested hin, and he saw the wavering gleam of a lantern on the tops of the furze bushes that grew on the fence near the gate. There was a clatter as of a spade falling on the road, and then he heard Ellen's laugh.

'Now, maybe, ye'll let me carry the can by myself. Ye've more than ye're able for with the spade and the lantern.'

Dan stood stiff and still to hear the rejoinder.

'The spade itself is more than I'm able for,' Rick O'Grady's voice replied; 'I guess it's seven years good since I handled a shovel, let alone made a pit of mangels. Faith, I'm as tired now as if I'd been buryin' me father !'

'Oh, indeed, then that's the pit !' Ellen stopped to laugh again. 'Them that sees it will know we were hard set for a workman !'

'Wouldn't I give satisfaction, afther all ? Wouldn't ye be content to let me work for ye ?'

The voice was softened and lowered, but Dan heard every word—heard, too, Ellen's answer :

'I'd be satisfied so long as the workman wouldn't complain.'

And Rick's, spoken with unmistakable meaning :

'Then I b'lieve ye have a servant that'd work for ye all yer life.'

The light of the lantern flared into the yard.

'The gate's open, I declare !' she said ; 'I wondher if Dan's back from the fair.'

As if in answer, the light fell with a leap on Dan himself, standing near the door in his white flannel coat, with his head thrust forward in the attitude of listening.

Ellen and Rick stopped short with startled exclamations, and at the same moment Rick's yellow terrier made a dash at what she doubtless believed to be an apparition, barking shrilly and vociferously to persuade herself and her master that she was not in the least alarmed.

'Yes, I'm back,' Dan called out; then, as the dog still circled barking round him, the pent-up feelings of the day found vent in a kick from his hobnailed boot that sent her shrieking back across the yard.

'What the devil right have you to kick my dog?' said Rick, putting down the spade and lantern, and coming striding across the yard towards the assailant.

'And what right have you or the dog

here ?' retorted Dan, inspired for the first
time in his life to courageous answer by that
strange stir and burning in his head.

'Oh, Dan!' cried Ellen, horror-struck.
'What are ye sayin' at all ? Sure, isn't
Misther O'Grady afther comin' here workin'
for us the whole evening !'

'Then I tell him we're well able to do
without him and his work!' shouted Dan,
losing all control of himself at Ellen's inter-
ference. 'He's a dommed spy, and I tell
him so to his face !' He raised his stick as if
he meant to strike at Rick, but before his
arm could fall, he found himself gripped by
the collar of his coat, and swung off his legs
on to his back in the dirt.

He lay so still for a moment that Ellen
thought he was dead, and ran to him with a
loud cry. At the same instant the cottage
door opened with a bang, and Mrs. Leonard
appeared, her hands covered with flour and

dough, and her face expressive of the utmost consternation.

' Who's hurt at all ?' she called out; ' glory be to God, Ellen ! was it you let that screech ? I thought ye were killed !' Then seeing in the half-light of the lantern Dan slowly getting on to his feet and picking up his hat, 'Arrah, musha what knocked ye there in the gutther, ye omadthawn ? Can't ye spake ? Is it dhrunk ye are ?'

' He put as infernal a lie on me as any man ever put !' said Rick heatedly, 'and raised his stick to me, and I threw him there the way he'd learn manners !'

' Is that the thruth ?' demanded the widow in formidable tones, going out and taking Dan by the arm.

He turned such a face upon her that even her tough nerves received a jar, it was so sickly, unbelievably white; and when he spoke his lips drew back and showed his

teeth with the grin of a furious caged
animal.

'I'll say it agin to him!' he said, stuttering
and shivering with the effort to express himself. 'He's spyin' on ye, and I know—I
know who's sent him to do it!'

'And I say again to ye,' replied Rick,
coming and standing straight in front of him,
'that ye're the infernalest liar in Ireland this
minute; and if it wasn't that ye'd not repay
what throuble a man 'd have in kickin' ye,
I'd make ye that ye'd be sorry for this the
longest day ye'll live!'

'Lave him alone!' vociferated Mrs. Leonard, her ready suspicion awake in a moment,
stretching out a thick floury arm to keep
Rick off. 'What is it, Dan Hurley? Spake
out now—he'll not touch ye.'

'I don't care whether he'll touch me or
not!' blustered Dan, warming under this
comfortable assurance; then with a sudden

inspiration, into which was concentrated the venom that was half choking him : ' Maybe he'll tell ye who it was was waitin' for him in the wood last Sunday, afther he leavin' this, an' went back in the boat with him !' He ended with a laugh that might have been taken from Caliban's *répertoire*, and that sent a baleful gleam into his light eyes, as, without turning his head, he moved them from the widow's face to Ellen's.

The pitfall opened before Rick with a suddenness that nearly sent him off his balance. To avoid the stammer or hesitation that would have ruined him, he was forced to pause before answering, and the three members of his tribunal appreciated each instant of delay, linking it to their own thoughts, with exultation, with angry conviction, and in one case with a painfully growing fear.

'I met Mrs. Donovan by chance, walking
in the wood that afternoon,' he said as quietly
as he could ; 'and I offered to row her home.
I suppose there's nothing very out-of-the-
way in that ?'

'No, indeed !' said Ellen, with a laugh—
whose kindliness had a little sickly ring in
it ; 'what's the harm in anyone giving a lift
to a friend, Dan ?'

'Oh, no harm at all !' said Mrs. Leonard,
an unctuous politeness falling with tropical
calm into her speech. 'Of coorse, Misther
O'Grady has a right to oblige his friends—
more than all, sich an old friend as Mrs.
Donovan !'

The widow had jumped to her conclusion
with characteristic recklessness, goaded by
pride, distrust, and, it must be admitted, by
the contingent disappointment of seeing
certain nebulous matrimonial ideas melt into
nothingness. Rick would have found it diffi-

cult to combat this alarming attitude, but Dan gave him no time.

'Go and look in yer cowhouse!' he said, with a gesture towards it, ' an' ye'll know what work Misther O'Grady and his friends have done for ye! There's yer nine heifers in it, and 'twould have been as good for them to have been in it all day. There wasn't one livin' crayture in the fair o' Cloonmore spoke to me, nor put a hand on the cattle to price them; they had no more considheration for me than if I was the dirt undher their feet.'

Mrs. Leonard flung her arms out in front of her, and struck her palms together.

'That God may not see flesh on them!' she burst out. 'An' may the day come when themselves 'll be beggin' the price of what'll fill their shtummuck from them that'll not give!'

'I saw the dommed ruffian that was tellin'

9

the people to boycott me,' went on Dan, his voice growing louder and wilder at every word. ' 'Twas John Donovan himself—there was nothin' brought him to the fair, only that. I declare to God he didn't buy nor sell a baste in it. An' who was it told him ye'd have cattle in it? Think now—who was it ye told last Sunday ye'd be sendin' them heifers to Cloonmore Fair to-day? Wasn't it to Rick O'Grady ye said it, when he came out here so nice and so natty in his Sunday clothes, tellin' ye he'd help ye, an' lettin' on to be coortin' Ellen, an' Mrs. Donovan waitin' for him in the wood below, till he'd tell her how he had ye med a fool of!' He flung his hat on the ground, and squared his left arm in front of his head, half in defiance, and half as if he expected to be attacked.

Rick stood quite still, his clenched hands hanging by his sides.

'Ye needn't be afraid,' he said; 'I'll not touch ye this time. But I'll tell ye, Mrs. Leonard, if ye believe the lies he's after tellin' ye, ye'll be turning away the only friend ye have left.'

With a great effort Mrs. Leonard recovered her sultry suavity of manner.

'I'd be sorry to part with such a good friend as ye've been to us; but I think I'd sooner have the price of me cattle than a friend like ye. I'm obliged to ye for the help ye give me, and I thrust in God He'll presarve every poor woman that's hard set like me, from sich help as that! Good-evenin' to ye, Misther O'Grady.' She bobbed a sort of curtesy to him, and turned towards the house.

Rick turned too, and marched straight to the gate, his anger too hot in him for reply. As he passed Ellen, he said 'Good-bye' in a hard, strained voice, and he felt it to be the final act of injustice that she made no answer.

As he turned into the lane an impulse, that he could not withstand, made him look back ; and he saw the three of them standing there, the light from the lantern on the ground shining up on them, and making Dan's face look diabolically triumphant.

It was at that moment that Ellen gathered strength to break away from her indecision and her daunting surroundings. She ran after Rick into the lane ; she gave him her hand, and said, with her soft voice quivering :

'Don't mind what they say. I know ye're a good friend to us—I'll never believe anything but that of ye. Good-bye !'

Then, before he could answer her, she had run back again to take the consequences of her action.

CHAPTER X.

ON THE HILLSIDE.

THE consequences were severe. Anyone could have told that, who saw Ellen the next morning, as she slowly climbed the hill at the back of her mother's house, with a basket of newly-washed linen on her head. Even the light southerly wind that rustled freshly through the furze-bushes brought only a faint snatch of colour to her pale face, and her transparent gray eyes had the pathetic brilliancy that only young eyes can have after bitter crying—the clear shining after much rain.

Ellen was not much more than eighteen,

and her mother's anger was still a very
terrible event to her, so that after the furious
outburst of it the night before, she had lain
awake, crying miserably and silently, while
her mother snored on implacably beside her ;
and when a delicately flashing sunrise had
called them both to their work, and she
found that she was to be treated with an
austere and gloomy aloofness, she felt, with
the touching, headlong despair of youth, that
she would rather die than bear all this un-
happiness.   It cannot, of course, be supposed
that she explained her own emotions to herself very intelligibly; that luxury, or torment,
whichever it is, is reserved for the cultured ;
but it is certain that when, last night, she lay
awake, in the thick darkness, with the tears
soaking into her pillow, and now, as she
took the basket from her head and put
it down on the short grass, the thought
that made the lump rise again in her

throat was of the injustice done to Rick O'Grady.

She spread out the clothes on the furze-bushes, and on a briary fence close by, moving to and fro on the hillside, with the sun shining on her yellow hair, and on the white linen that lay all around her like snow. Curlew and plover were swooping and whistling high in the dazzling air above her, and a couple of crows sat on a scraggy thornbush half-way down the hill, and debated hoarsely as to whether all this white stuff that was being strewn about so carefully was likely to be good to eat. Ellen was in no hurry to return to the storm-fraught atmosphere of the cottage; the sun was warm, and the silence was soothing, and she lingered over her task of spreading and opening out the linen. Even after she had no further excuse for delay, and had picked up her basket to go home, she stood with it

held against her hip with one hand, shading
her eyes with the other as she looked down
over her mother's farm, at the arm of the
harbour below, and the dangerous mud-flats
of Scariff Bay, gleaming bare in the low tide.
There was the little landing-place where
Rick had fastened up his boat, with the
golden-brown seaweed weltering in the sun
on the rocks in front of it; her eye followed
the line of the river up to the ivy-grown old
mill by the bridge; that was where she said
good-bye to him that first day; and there,
down in the brown field by the river, she
could see the place where they had made the
pit of mangels together last night.   The
pain was coming again about her throat, and
the mist gathering before her eyes, when she
heard, as if it dropped from the blue sky
above her, a voice calling her name.

She turned, and with her hand still
shading her eyes, looked up and down the

rocky hill, her heart beating loudly in her ears. The brown outline of the hill-top against the blue was jagged with great loose boulders, and between a couple of these she saw Rick O'Grady's well-known figure standing. He waved his cap to her, and with an ecstatic change of mood she waved her hand in return. At once he disappeared from against the sky-line, and with feelings in which alarm and delight were about equally blended, she watched his active figure coming lightly down the heathery slope towards her. She stood motionless as he neared her ; somehow the delight was fading out of her, and fear wholly asserted itself as she saw that his fresh face looked pale and grave. He took her hand and pressed it hard before he spoke.

'Ellen,' he said, 'I couldn't sleep last night thinking of the way yer mother treated me, and wondering would she make ye believe that lie the way she did herself.'   His brisk American accent had quite deserted him, and his voice was low and troubled. ' If I'd known what was to happen your cattle at the fair, I'd have gone there myself and bought them. On me soul, I would, and you might believe me.'

His earnestness, and the evident pain in his blue eyes, made Ellen more than ever ashamed for her mother's ingratitude.

' Me mother's very hasty that way,' she answered confusedly ; ' she believes anything a person will tell her sometimes, and she was that distracted like about the cattle——' She paused, seeking desperately for some further palliating motive on her mother's part.

' I think she had a right to believe me as soon as that—that—' he checked himself—' as soon as Dan.   But it's not your mother I'm thinking of.   Tell me now, Ellen, do *you* believe all they said of me ?'

The same passion of faith in him that had overcome her last night thrilled her through and through again.

'Oh no, no, I don't—in troth I don't,' she replied with such an earnestness that the colour came glowing to her cheeks; 'it's you I believe, and I don't mind what Dan nor anyone said.'

Her eyes kindled with a brilliant light, and as she looked up at Rick with her hair stirred about her forehead by the breeze, he thought her the loveliest sight he had ever seen in his life. For a moment the only possible answer seemed to be to put his arms about her and tell her that as long as she believed in him he did not care what anyone else thought of him. But an unusual timidity and self-distrust checked him on the verge of this summary proceeding; there was such an unconsciousness about her faith in him that he felt afraid to venture any shock to it.

'So long as you'll trust me I'm satisfied,'
he said, his eyes delaying long on her
face. A cloud drifted across the sun, and
threw the hillside into sudden shadow; a
seagull wailed, swooping low over their
heads, and in a moment the warmth went
out of the wind. The glow went out of
Ellen's heart too, and all the difficulties
that beset her seemed to press up darkly
about her—foremost and most formidable
among them the thought of her mother's
furious indignation if this meeting with Rick
were ever found out.

'I must go home,' she said anxiously; 'if
Dan sees you, or me mother, I don't know
what'd happen me.'

Rick looked over the top of the fence down
to the farm below.

'Oh, it's all right,' he said, lowering his
voice, however; 'your mother's digging potatoes in the field by the house, and she'll

never see us up here. I've something I must tell you,' he went on, leaning his elbows against the fence and looking at her. 'This boycotting that's been got up against your mother is just a put-up job of Donovan's. I had a letter this morning from a friend in X——,' mentioning the principal town of the neighbourhood, 'and it showed me very plain that them that's in authority there had no hand in this business. They know as well as me it was no question of rent made James Mahony give up that farm, for all he owed three years' rent to his landlord; but he was ashamed to stop in the counthry after—after —any way, the rent was the excuse he put on it. Tell me now, was there ever any quarrel between your mother and Donovan?'

The interest of the subject had revived the practical tendencies of Rick's nature, and Ellen suddenly felt herself immeasurably the inferior of this smart, business-like young man. She came near calling him 'sir' as she replied :

'I don't remember that they ever were very great with one another; an' I've often heard me mother say that since ever the time she took Dan for a servant-boy Misther Donovan would never lose a chance to do her a bad turn.'

Rick pulled his moustache thoughtfully.

'And was Donovan so set as all that to have that beauty for himself?'

Ellen turned her head to one side, and put the corner of her apron over her mouth to conceal the irrepressible smile which this idea called forth.

'Oh, Misther O'Grady!' she said, with a sidelong glance to see if Rick was as much amused as she was, 'sure you know very well that John Donovan got the Hurleys' farm, and hates the very name o' them. Sure it was charity made me mother take poor Dan the time his mother went to the workhouse, and Mr. Donovan was mad for he not going into the house with the mother.'

'Angry, was he ? H'm, that's strange !' Rick commented, and fell again into silence.

Ellen looked up at his abstracted face, and then thought of her mother, digging potatoes in the field below.

'I think I'll have to go down now,' she said ; 'maybe I'll be wanted. Dan has to be back in Drimnahoon now every day, minding the cattle, and there's not one to do a hand's turn about the place, only meself and me mother. 'Oh !' she cried, with a bitter realization of their hopeless plight, 'God help us if it's Misther Donovan that has us boycotted this way ! He's too sthrong for poor people like us.'

She turned away to pick up her basket again, and this time Rick did not resist the impulse that took possession of him. He gathered her slight figure into his arms, and lifted her frightened, bewildered face to his own.

'Are ye frightened now, asthore?' he whispered. No answer from Ellen, except something that might have been a sob. 'I know well ye're not. Ye wouldn't be frightened when ye know I love ye that way that I'd die for ye before anyone should hurt ye.'

The cloud-shadow swept away from over the hill, and the sunlight turned her yellow hair to gold, and swam in the depths of her wet gray eyes as she lifted them at last and gave her lips to her first lover.

CHAPTER XI.

AN OUTCAST.

ANYONE who had felt the freshness of the wind on Drimnahoon, and seen from its heights the brightness of the sea, would marvel that a man who had once known those things could endure his life in a filthy lodging-house in the slums of a small inland town. It was not, therefore, to be wondered at that after James Mahony had been for about two months the occupant of a room in a back lane of Cloonmore, the last remnants of his vigour and self-respect seemed to have slipped from him. He had felt himself to have fallen low when he took the room, and

began to work as a day-labourer wherever he
could get employment; now, as he sat with
his gaunt frame huddled on a low wooden
bedstead, and chewed the hunch of bread and
drank the mug of muddy-looking tea that
formed his invariable diet, he had lost all
sense of degradation or incongruity in his
surroundings.

His little son, a creature like a Japanese
caricature of a frog, was perched on a painted
wooden box, whose gaudy, grimy labels testi-
fied that it had made the journey to America
and back. The signs of Transatlantic travel
and sojourn were on the boy as well as the
box; in the wizened precocity of his yellow
face, and the twang in his shrill voice as
he asked his father for another 'sup o'
tay.'

'There's no more for ye,' replied Mahony
shortly, putting away his mug on a shelf,
beneath which a pair of trousers and an old

coat hung on a peg, and walking to the window.

The child accepted the situation by turning up his mug and sucking the last sugary dregs from it ; while his father, stooping down to the level of the little window, rubbed one of its panes comparatively clean with his coat-sleeve, and looked out into the lane. ` There was nothing to be seen there except a couple of old hags, red-eyed and ragged, who were telling each other in a loud drunken bawl the events of the day's begging ; but James Mahony remained there, leaning his big muscular hands on the sill of the window, and looking out into the failing light.

He was thinking of how, on an evening like this in the November of last year, he had driven his own horse out of Cloonmore in the smart new outside car that he had just bought to please his wife, and that he had

10—2

spent more money on than he cared to tell her. He had been married to her then for eight anxious years—years in which he had tried by alternate severity and spoiling to win the heart or break the spirit of a girl who had married a man thirty years older than herself; a marriage that had been made on the financial principles that govern the alliances of crowned heads, and of the Irish peasantry. He had in his own way done his best; but he was a rash, sanguine man, given to theorizing and to a pugnacious belief in his own theories, and his extravagant mismanagement of his farm was of a piece with his treatment of his wife. She was a Hegarty, of the same violent clan as the Widow Leonard, whose near kinswoman she was; and though more subtle in her methods than that imperious lady, she was equally determined on having her own way.

Disaster of a double kind crept slowly

towards him, though he would not believe in
its advance till one April evening, when he
came home from work, and his child, paddling
gleefully in the duck-pond, screamed to him
that his mammy had gone away on the new
car, and was gone to Cloonmore with Tom
Barrett driving her.

James Mahony went into his house with
some presentiment of coming evil; it was
empty, the fire on the hearth had gone out,
and lying on the table, with its brass-bound
jaws wide open, was the old leather purse
that had held all his ready money.

It seemed to him afterwards that that had
been the worst moment, but it was perhaps
the waiting, the half-expectancy, while the
soft spring night drew in round him, that
had been the hardest to endure. The lad
from Cloonmore, who at nine o'clock brought
the car home, scarcely dared to give his
message to the silent old man, who came out

in the moonlight to meet him as he rattled into the yard. Nothing but the luxury of telling bad news upheld him during his narration of how Tom Barrett and Mrs. Mahony had told him to drive home the car from the station, and how he had seen them going off by the train that was to meet the American steamer at Queenstown ; and, in conclusion, would Mr. Mahony give him a shilling for driving over the car ?

James Mahony's only answer was a look so dreadful that the boy waited for no further reply, and making the best of his way back to Cloonmore, spread through the town the piquant tale of how old James Mahony's wife had gone away to America with his farm-servant, and that James Mahony himself was like to kill him when he told him the news.

After this the tenant of Drimnahoon seemed to live in a black rain of misfortune.

Somehow the fact of the robbery of his money leaked out, and quickened the apprehensions of his many creditors among the shopkeepers of Rossbrin and Cloonmore ; and their knowledge that his rent for three Novembers had remained unpaid made them not unreasonably anxious to get what they could before there would be nothing of the carcase left to devour. James Mahony endured on in silence for a month or more ; a still, fierce, brooding man, with a heart that was being slowly eaten through by pain and shame, as worms eat through a log. He took no notice of the letters from his various creditors, hired no workmen, did nothing, in fact, beyond tending his child and the live stock on the farm. The ' May gale ' of rent came due ; but when the agent came in person to threaten this defaulting tenant with all the penalties of the law, he took little good of his visit. The sleepless rage

found its outlet, and the agent drove away
with Mahony's threats and curses sounding
in his ears, and his mind made up to post a
writ to the tenant of Drimnahoon without
further delay.

He might have spared himself the trouble.
James Mahony sold all his stock next day
at the big May fair in Cloonmore, and two
days afterwards he and his boy left Drimnahoon in the gray of the morning, and set
forth for the country which to an Irishman
means either wealth or oblivion—whichever
he is in search of—America.

He told no one of his intention, and left
his landlord and his other creditors to fight it
out amongst them as best they could.   Perhaps his object was merely to escape from
the shame that clung to him like a garment;
perhaps low in his bewildered mind there
lurked a hope that in the country where
everything seemed possible some chance of

vague terrific revenge might be put in his way.

Whatever the motive, it is certain that he did not find what he wanted there. He was too old a man to fill the gap in his life with any fresh interest or enterprise; and in the roar and press of the big city in which he found himself he thought more of the green fields and the quiet life that he had foregone than of present advantage or future vengeance. The child pined in the scorching heat of the New York summer, and he himself began to feel that he was old, and unable to compete in this strenuous grapple with fortune. He had still money enough to take him home again, and after one or two blazing Sunday afternoons, on which he walked with little Tim to watch the start of a big liner, the craving for his own country mastered him, and he took ship for Ireland.

He had slipped out of Cloonmore like a

ghost, and like a ghost he came back to it, to find, like many another ghost, perhaps, that the place and things in which all his thoughts had centred had entered on another phase of existence in which he had no part. His creditors had shared amongst them the money brought by the sale of his tenant-right, and the cattle of his nearest neighbour throve on the grass that had been his. The passion for home turned to a proud sullen avoidance of old acquaintances, and a jealous hatred of those who were prospering where he had failed. He had spent all he had to get back to Drimnahoon, and he found himself obliged to remain in Cloonmore, falling in all ways from bad to worse—drifting like a wrecked ship that is going to pieces on the rocks outside its own harbour.

The November evening became grayer and darker, and the people in the house opposite lighted their lamp. Mahony turned from the window with an inarticulate growl, and felt along the shelf for the matches. As he struck one and applied it to the wick of his chimneyless lamp, there was a loud knock at the door, and before permission to enter was given, it was pushed open wide enough to admit the imposing figure of Mr. John Donovan.

CHAPTER XII.

MEPHISTOPHELES.

'WELL, James, how are ye?' began Mr. Donovan, in his pompous, unemotional voice. 'I'm a little late, maybe, but I had business the other side of the town.'

'Good-evenin',' responded Mahony, with a surly apathy of manner that belied the excitement in his sunken eyes, and the twitching of the muscles of his face. He hung the lamp on a nail and turned to the child, who, still sitting on the box, was staring at the visitor with unrestrained curiosity.

'Go down out o' that and play in the sthreet,' said his father, in the loud bullying

voice reserved by men of his class for children
and animals. 'Be off now!' as the child
lingered on his way to the door.

Mahony shut it after him, and took up
his original position on the bed, Donovan
having, after an inspection of the solitary
chair, preferred to establish himself on the
box in the window.

'Well, them's very busy times,' he remarked
—'very busy. I don't know when I've had
so much to do, one way or th' other, as I
have now.'

'Well, and is that what ye've come here
to say?' asked Mahony morosely. 'I lost half
me day's work the way I'd be here before ye.'

Donovan rolled a surprised eye upon his
host, not so much in resentment as in diag-
nosis.

'The old man has a dhrop taken,' he said
to himself. 'Well, no harm, no harm.
Well, James,' he continued aloud, 'I'm sorry

I was delayed ; but business first, pleasure
aftherwards.   Ha, ha!' he wheezed an
unctuous laugh, and pulled out a fat pocket-
book, from which, after some deliberation, he
selected a one-pound note. ' I wanted to bring
ye this,' he said, slowly smoothing its dirty
creases out on his knee.   ' Ye were sayin' ye
wanted some sort of an advance the last time
I was here ; ye can take ye're own time to
pay me afther ye get the situation we were
speaking about.'

Mahony stretched out his hand for the
note, and put it in his pocket without a
word.

' I didn't see ye now since the fair,' Donovan went on.   ' That was a pretty good fair,
mind ye, and a terrible high price for young
cattle, barrin' a few.'

The old man suddenly opened his great
jaws and laughed.

' Begor' ye had thim well soorted that

day!' he said. ' Ye're a smart man, John Donovan.'

' Them was nine fine bastes of the Widow Leonard's was dhriven home,' continued Donovan, placidly ignoring Mahony's remark. ' There's no betther feeding in the counthry than what there is in Drimnahoon, and them bastes had the appairance of it.' His brown swimming eye rested steadily on Mahony. ' But no man should know that betther than yerself, Jim, and that's the reason, as I was sayin' to ye the last time I seen ye, that as soon as that farm falls into my hands I'll be well satisfied to put ye into it, and make a dairy farm of it.'

' And what's to make Margaret Leonard quit out of that ?' Mahony asked contemptu- ously. ' If hell was to open undher her feet in it, she'd stay there !'

' Maybe so,' replied Donovan, with his in- describable accent of patient superiority. ' But it's not thrusting to hell the agent'll be when he'll ax her for the rent, and she'll not have it.   I know well it was them heifers she was depending on to pay the rent, and b'lieve you me, Burke 'll be apt to be pretty smart with her.   He's had throuble enough out of Dhrim-nahoon this year.'

The old man got up and walked once or twice up and down the room, as if his long legs were cramped.   Then he opened the door and looked out into the passage, and shutting it again, came and stood in front of Donovan, with a hot sparkle in his hollow eyes, and his hands clenching and unclenching them-selves as they hung at his sides.

' Throuble !' he repeated ; ' who knows what throuble is as well as me ?   What throuble had he to drive to me doore to give me his ordhers ?   By —— ! if I'd had a gun in me hand that day, he'd be rottin' in his grave this minute !'

'Well, indeed, an' ye shouldn't be blemt to feel that way,' said Donovan sympathetically; 'it's a hard thing to see a poor man put out of his little place for the lewcre of a few pounds, and ye may be sure, James, I'll not be the one that'll press ye for the little matther of money that was between us when ye left Dhrimnahoon.'

'Ye got the haff of it whatever,' growled Mahony.

'Certainly, of coorse!' with admirable politeness; 'I'm not disputin' that. But supposin' now, James, that I was to get that farm, and I was to put you back into it to manage it, and you havin' the name of bein' the tenant,' all these points emphasized by the striking of a heavy forefinger into the palm of the other hand, 'wouldn't that be betther for ye than to be the way y'are? Ye'd have yer own share out of the profits, and as for any small matther of money ye may

owe to me or any other one in Rossbrin, if
the people thought ye were to be reinstated
back in the farm, they'd have a bonfire before
ye in it, and *cead mille failthe !*   Bedad they
would! there isn't one of them doesn't hate
the idaya of a land-grabber !' Mr. Donovan
paused, a little out of breath from the unwonted effort to be hearty and benevolent.

Mahony's sullen, uncertain eye rested on
him suspiciously, his eyebrows meeting and
his underlip dropping as he tried to con-
centrate his thoughts on the question as to
where in this attractive scheme lay the
disadvantage to himself. He felt that it
must be there, but he could not for the life
of him see it, and had to rest content with
saying:

'It's aisy talkin'! I suppose ye think ye
have nothin' to do but to ax the farm of the
widda and she'll give it to ye!'

Donovan had at once appreciated Mahony's

difficulty and its cause, and saw also how well his plan had held water. He determined to lose no more time.

'If ye're satisfied with what I'm afther sayin' to ye,' he said slowly, 'and if ye'll stand by me the way I'll stand by you, I think ye'll see the day that ye'll get that farm without axing, because she'll be glad to be shut of it.'

Mahony stared at him, compelled to a belief in his power.

'I'll shtand by ye!' he said excitedly; 'ye know that well! I'd shtand by the divil himself if he'd put Margaret Hegarty off me land!' The very mention of the name that had been his wife's seemed to madden him like the cut of a whip. 'Damn it! Spake out, man, and tell me what ye want! Do ye want more of them heifers killed?'

'Hold yer whisht!' said Donovan angrily. 'Do ye want the neighbours to come to

listen to ye ?   I never told ye to kill one of
the widow's heifers ; ye'll please to remember
that.'

'I'll swear on the Bible I'd never have
done it if it wasn't for ye !' replied Mahony,
sinking his voice to a fierce whisper ; 'and
much good it done afther !'

'I tell ye what it done,' said Donovan,
'that there isn't one in Margaret Leonard's
house that isn't thrimblin' for their lives this
minute.   I have the manes of knowin' that.
I know for a fact they have their beds dhrew
in undher the windows for fear they'd get a
shot in the night !'   He struck his open hand
on his leg.   'But what I was goin' to mention before was that maybe the widow will
make some sort of a thry to fatten them
heifers and send them to Cork, or maybe
Liverpool.   She's a parsevaring woman, and
there's a gieat price for cattle in England.
She has good feedin' for them, too—the best.

There's no finer rick of hay in the counthry than what she has.' He looked up into the savage, expectant face of the old man. ' It's a fine rick, James, and it'll stand her the whole winther, unless'—he waited a second, and looked, as it were, absently at the ceiling— ' unless there was any accident happened it.'

Mahony stooped towards him, a grin spreading hideously over his face. Then he swung himself back and laughed, clapping his hands against his thighs.

' That'll do ! That'll do !' he said, stamping from one foot to the other, and rubbing his hands. ' Say no more now !'

John Donovan rose to his feet and buttoned up his coat.

' Well, James !' he said in his expressionless voice, ' I must be for the road, and it's a cold night. Ye might as well come and have a dhrop of somethin' at Mullins's.'

It had grown quite dark by this time, and

Mahony held the lamp at the door to light
his visitor down the dirty broken staircase.
He stood there till Donovan's cautious and
shuffling descent was ended ; then he
replaced his lamp on the shelf, and putting
the box of matches in his pocket, followed
Donovan into the lane.

CHAPTER XIII.

A HEART AND ITS BITTERNESS.

THE small house that Rick had taken for himself in Rossbrin possessed three attributes that at once placed it on the pinnacle of respectability. It had two stories, it kept its hall-door closed, and its lower window had a wire-blind. This last, indeed, had been for a time looked on by the community as a mark of almost offensive exclusiveness in the young man whom they remembered in his lawless youth as the scourge of the quiet and respectable members of the community, and by no means a credit to his father, an ancient and peaceable naval pensioner. But

with their slow recognition of his success
came a respect for what was regarded as an
eccentricity of genius, and the wire-blind
became in their eyes as much a symbol of
business and concealed riches, as if it bore
the four golden letters of the word ' Bank.'

What it did conceal was a dingy, comfortable room, with little in it besides a big table,
a big desk, and a big armchair, in which, on the
afternoon which Mr. Donovan had selected for
his drive into Cloonmore, Rick O'Grady was
sitting. The remains of his solitary dinner
were still on the table in untempting array,
and the plate from which the little yellow dog
had licked her master's leavings was on the
rug, surrounded by the potato-skins which
she had contemptuously nosed from out of
the mess as unfit for a lady of delicate appe-
tite. Rick had a pipe in his mouth, and a
note-book in his hand, the open page of the
latter thickly covered with entries and figures

in a very clear round hand. Its purport was of fish and fish barrels and consignments, and might well have accounted for the anxious frown with which its owner was staring at the white and brown diamonds of wall - paper opposite him.

He had sat there quite still for some time, the note-book open at the same page, and his teeth gripping the mouthpiece of his pipe, which had gone out from lack of attention. But still the difficulty that his mind was trying in twenty different ways to penetrate remained acute and intact as ever. Fish and their transits had no place in it. It was, to put it in the form in which it presented itself to Rick's mind, the problem of how best to convince the neighbourhood that Mr. John Donovan was a liar and a traitor.

In his own mind he was certain of it ; he knew that it was the personal influence of the gombeen man that had created and bolstered up the boycotting of the Widow Leonard ; but in a case of this kind, where most of the members of the League were debtors, either present or possible, of its President, and self-interest made every one of them ready to declare that he was acting from conviction, an empty denunciation would be worse than useless. He could bring no proof, he could allege no motive ; who would believe him if he said that all this large, troublesome machinery had been set going by Donovan to gratify his private spite against Dan Hurley ? And yet what other motive could he have ? That was the point that kept Rick at bay, and blocked the way of all further plans.

These in themselves were simple enough. He meant to marry Ellen Leonard, with or without her mother's consent ; that was the one star that shone clear to him out of dark uncertainties ; but being in the main a prudent and practical young man, he preferred,

in the first instance, to set himself straight
in the eyes not only of the world, but of that
redoubtable adversary, his future mother-in-
law. Once or twice his heart swelled fool-
ishly as his fancy took the bit in its teeth,
and he imagined some impossible moment in
which his single act of valour should save
Ellen and all belonging to her from some
equally impossible climax of destruction ; and
each time he returned upon the ignoble reality
that he had for the last two days been obliged
to skulk and skirt behind the Scariff hedges
and banks, waiting for the moment when luck
or strategy should enable Ellen to elude the
maternal eye.

From this point it was but a short and
seductive step to blissful reflection on Ellen's
many adorable qualities ; and he was for the
third time beginning to live over again his
last meeting with her, when there came a
single thump at the knocker of his hall door—

a liberty instantly and furiously challenged by
Colleen, the yellow terrier.

Rick opened the door himself, silencing
Colleen's remonstrances with a deft side-kick,
and Mick, the boy from the hotel at the top
of the hill, handed him a letter.   Rick went
back to his sitting-room ; he opened the blue
commercial envelope with a sense of interrup-
tion and uneasiness, and read the few words
written in violet ink on the thin, shiny
paper.

' DEAR MR. O'GRADY,

' If you could come across to the
hotel now, I would be glad to speak to
you.

' H. DONOVAN.'

He stood for a minute twisting the letter
impatiently about in his fingers.

' What's she up to now, I wonder !' he said
to himself.

Then he put the letter in the fire, and, picking up his cap and stick, went out of the house.

The afternoon was rough and dark, and the south - west wind was bringing large gloomy companies of clouds in from the sea. ' This wind ought to bring the boats in,' thought Rick as he climbed the stiff rise of the street. ' I'll tell her I have to go on up to the look-out before the light goes, to see are they coming in.'

With the comforting thought that he now held in reserve a means of escape, he knocked at the private entrance of the hotel, and was presently conducted by tortuous passages to Harriet's sitting-room.

They had not met since the Sunday before, when he had rowed her home in his boat, and he thought with no small anxiety that the part he had played on that occasion might be a difficult one to sustain. But even as he

shook hands with her, he was aware that the
atmosphere was charged with electricity, and
that in the three days since he had seen her
the barometer had dropped from 'set fair' to
'stormy.' He could, however, scarcely have
told how he knew this. There was an almost
angelic sweetness in Harriet's manner as she
begged him to sit down, and hoped she had
not been very troublesome to him in asking
him to come up the hill. Rick, as in duty
bound, assured her that the trouble was a
pleasure, and inwardly wished he had not
been at home when Mrs. Donovan's note
arrived.

'I wouldn't have asked you to come,' went
on Harriet, as they sat down on each side of
the fire, 'only for Mr. Donovan being in
Cloonmore, and I was glad to have the
chance to speak to you privately.'

'Well, that's all right!' struck in Rick
vaguely with a nervous laugh.

' I'm told,' pursued Harriet unsmilingly,
' that you're putting yerself in the way of
great danger.' She paused with her dark
eyes full on Rick.

He managed to laugh again, and said,
twirling his cap carelessly,

' That's news. Who told ye that ?'

Harriet did not fail to notice that her
words had been startling, but she made the
mistake that a woman in a higher class of
life would not have made in a similar case—
she thought she had frightened him about his
own personal safety.

' It's no matter who told me,' she said.
' I heard it from more than one, any way.'

' Well, ye might tell me what they said, I
suppose. It's a funny thing to tell a man
he's in danger, and not to tell him why,'
returned Rick, still affecting to treat the
affair as a joke, but mentally turning up his
shirt-sleeves.

' I think ye might know it without me tellin' ye ; any way, the Land League knows why, and, maybe, they'll tell ye the story quicker than I could.'

Rick saw the light twinkle on the beaded front of her dress with the quick rise and fall of her bosom.

'Why, Harriet,' he said laughingly, ' I never knew till now ye were such a hot Leaguer. I suppose ye'll be boycottin' me next; and then what would I do ?'

' I think ye'd do very well!' broke out Harriet, the first rift showing in the smooth volcanic surface; ' so long as ye can go to the Widow Leonard's and do her dirty work for her, it's little ye care to come here I'

' And was it from yer husband ye got that story ?' asked Rick, temporizing still, but feeling determined and dangerous.

I know more about ye than ever my husband knows,' she said, flashing her eyes upon him with sudden meaning. ' He knows enough, and plenty, but if he heard all I have to tell him, maybe ye'd be sorry.'

Rick sprang up.

' Look here, Harriet,' he said roughly, ' I'll stand no more of this fooling ; what I do is my own affair, and not yours, nor Donovan's neither ; but, in the name of God, if ye have anything sensible to say to me, spake out !'

Harriet sat erect in her chair, her face dead white, and her hands knotted together in her lap.

' I'm much obliged to ye for tellin' me I'm a fool, but, maybe, some day ye'll be sorry ye didn't take a fool's advice, and give up keeping company with them that's boycotted.'   .

' Well, if they are boycotted,' retorted Rick, playing his best card, ' it's only yer husband knows the reason for it, for the Land League doesn't !'

Harriet was silenced by surprise and consternation.   Fond as Mr. Donovan was of
his wife, he thought but meanly of women as
political confidantes ; but it happened that in
this matter Harriet's intuition and shrewd-
ness had made her independent of what he
chose to tell her, and she knew quite enough
of his schemes for Drimnahoon to tremble at
Rick's nearness to the truth.

'Sure, all Rossbrin knows as well as I do
that James Mahony ran away out of his farm,
and left it there,' continued Rick ; ' I don't see
that's any reason against anyone else taking
it.'

'Oh, indeed !' sneered Harriet, pulling herself together for the delivery of her final
taunt, 'ye've changed yer tune a good deal
since the evenings ye used to sit here, so
pleasant and friendly, drinking yer glass, and
tellin' John " land-grabbers was the curse of
the counthry "!   But that was before ye were

took on as servant-boy to make the pit of
mangels at Scariff! Ha, ha! I know all
about it, ye see!' She ended with a burst of
shrill hysterical laughter.

Then she had set a spy on him! It was
Rick's turn to be staggered now. He looked
down on her as she leaned back with a
quiver in her lips already beginning to mock
their own unreal laughter, and felt in the
midst of his own perplexities a kind of
horror in the thought that this spiteful,
treacherous woman could ever have been the
girl that he had wasted all his heart on.

'Well, Harriet,' he said bitterly, ' ye treated
me bad once, but I never thought that ye'd
sarve me this way.'

There was no light in the room except the
feeble flicker of the fire, and he did not see at
first that she had put her hands over her face
as he spoke. ' I'll say good-bye to ye now,'
he said, turning from her, when the unex-

pected sound of a strangling sob made him stop with a new astonishment.

In a moment her sobs came so thick that the words she was trying to frame were caught from her over and over again.

'Oh, Rick——' she gasped at length; 'don't—don't go.'

He came to her side in spite of himself.

'What do ye want of me?' he said more gently; 'why, what ails ye at all, Harriet?'

'I never meant to treat ye badly,' she said, the tears streaming through her fingers. 'It was only to warn ye there's them against ye that would think little to kill ye.' Her head sank forward in her hands till it rested on her knees, and he heard her moan to herself: 'Oh, what would I do! what would I do!'

Rick was not more than human; he stooped over her, feeling both touched and flattered, and putting his hand on her heaving shoulder, said very kindly :

'Ah, now, Harriet, don't cry that way; sure there's no harm will happen me.'

The handle of the door was turned, and Rick started violently back as Mr. Donovan's head was thrust in.

'Are ye there, Harriet?' he said in an excited whisper.

Harriet sat up.

'Yes, I am,' she replied, steadying her voice with astonishing self-control.

'Well, see here,' he went on, evidently not noticing Rick, who was standing in the deep shadow behind Harriet's chair, 'I want ye to hurry and get a bit of supper for old James Mahony in here; and don't let on that he's in the house. Be smart about it now, like a good girl. I dropped him outside the town, and he'll be here in a minute.'

'Very good,' replied Harriet; and this time not all her care could keep a suspicious catch out of her low, even voice.

But Donovan did not notice it.

'Well, hurry now,' he repeated; 'I have to get in a lot of things out of the trap.' He shut the door, and they heard him go into the shop.

Rick came forward with the inevitably guilty air of a man who feels himself to be in a false position. Harriet caught his arm and pushed him towards the door.

'He'd kill me if he thought ye were here!' she whispered; 'don't say a word, and I'll let ye out before he comes out of the shop.' She opened the door softly and crept out into the passage.

He followed her through the same windings, now pitch-dark, by which he had come in; and as she went before him he heard once or twice the slight shuddering, drawing-in of her breath that told of the interrupted tempest. A faint light came in through the fanlight over the door, and he could just make out the white glimmer of her face, when, with her hand on the latch, she turned towards him.

'Don't be afraid I'll tell John what I'm after sayin' to ye; but, oh! for God's sake take care!' Then, with a trembling effort: 'I didn't know rightly what I was at awhile ago; don't be angry.'

He did not forgive her, but some impulse of pity and remembrance came over him; he knew his own power and was half ashamed of it, and with a man's reliance on an act rather than a word of kindness, he bent down and hurriedly kissed her cheek.

He walked quickly down the hill to his own house, thinking uncomfortably of that last moment of his interview, and pondering deeply over all that had gone before it. He would have been less puzzled, on at least one point, had he known that about an hour ago Dan Hurley, slouching away from the post-office, where he had been posting a letter for his mistress, was followed by Mick with an intimation that he was wanted by Mrs. Donovan, and had subsequently held low and long converse with her over the counter of the hotel and a liberal pint of porter.

CHAPTER XIV.

WHEN the Rossbrin boats came in that evening, running up to their moorings before the
fresh wind, they brought with them the
largest take of mackerel they had had since
the beginning of the month. It was long
past dark before the last glittering basketful
had been landed, and the little crowd of men
and women who were waiting on the pier to
begin the serious business of cleaning and
salting made up their minds to being out of
their beds until at least four o'clock in the
morning, when the results of their night's

work would have to be started to catch the
early train at Cloonmore.

At ten o'clock the workers were in full
swing. There was a line of tables up the
middle of the pier, each with its paraffin lamp
smoking and flaring in the partial shelter of a
fish-box, and each with its wild Rembrandtish
group of women splitting the innumerable
mackerel, and rubbing lavish fistfuls of coarse
gray salt into each, before it was flung to the
men to be packed into barrels. The lamps
shone fantastically on the double row of
intent faces, on the quickly moving arms of
the women, crimsoned to the elbows, on the
tables, varnished with the same colour, and on
the cold silvery heaps of fish. The dark
hollow of the night seemed impenetrable
beyond this island of light and movement;
the frail young moon that had just shown
above the trees of the Trahartha woods when
Rick left the hotel had set long before, and

the only stars that had not been blotted out by the clouds were those that twinkled at the mastheads of the fishing-boats in the middle of the harbour.

The work was too strenuous and hurried to admit of much conversation on the part of those engaged in it, but the usual loafers hung about on the pier, prepared to smoke and talk till morning if necessary. Prominent and most jovial among these loiterers was Mr. John Donovan, who had, contrary to his usual practice, condescended to stroll down from the hotel to see what sort of business his friend Rick O'Grady was doing. That, at least, was the reason he gave as he leaned against a mooring-post and affably discussed with Rick the prospects of the fishing - season. The latter found these friendly attentions rather oppressive. They came incongruously after what he had just heard from Harriet of the esteem in which

he was held by the local Land League, and
instead of replying appropriately to the
genialities of its President, his mind was
disturbed by wonderings as to what they
portended.　He felt angry and ashamed at
the thought that a few hours before he had
crept from this man's house like a thief.
He had up to that last moment, at all events,
done nothing that he need be ashamed of,
and even that foolishness had been the consequence of having allowed himself to be
hustled off in that absurd way.　He groaned
in spirit when he thought of Harriet, and
what he stigmatized to himself as ' her
nonsense,' and he stood there gnawing his
moustache, with his cap thrust over his eyes,
while Donovan prosed on sapiently beside
him, apparently not noticing his preoccupa-
tion, or perhaps setting it down to an
incessant attention to the workers and their
business.

'They're workin' well, Misther O'Grady,' observed a fisherman, lounging up to them. 'But I think the rain 'll have ye bet, and we're near plenty of it. The tide 'll be ebbing in another hour, and I'm thinking it's the most it'll do to hold up till then.'

'Bedad, Dinny, it'll be a bad job for me if it doesn't hold dry for another couple of hours.' Rick turned his back on the line of blazing lamps as he spoke, and looked up into the blackness of the sky. 'That's a queer light over there back o' the woods!' he exclaimed; 'ye'd think it was the moon rising only that she set an hour ago.'

The men standing by him turned also, and stared at a faint glow perceptible in the sky over the Trahartha woods.

'Moon!' said Dinny Macarthy, 'that's no moon. It's liker a fire.' Even as he spoke there came a red pulsation in the glow. 'Be the powers above!' he shouted, 'it's the woods is on fire!'

In an instant every creature on the pier was gazing at the northern sky, and a chorus of excited voices was echoing his words.

''Tis the woods, sure enough,' said Donovan; 'and the art of man 'll not save them if that's the case.'

'Get out a boat!' called out another man; 'we can't see what it is at all till we're round the point.'

As he spoke a big man came plunging through the crowd towards the slip where the boats were hauled up.

'Hurry now!' he shouted; 'sure the wind's west, and maybe if we got there in time it wouldn't spread.'

'What's the good of that, ye fool?' Donovan called out. 'D'ye think ye can put it out with yer hat? What business is it of ours if every stick in it was burnt, and the man that owns it, too ? If he wouldn't live in the counthry and mind his place, let him lose it and be d——d to him !'

There was a sycophantic laugh or two of approval at Mr. Donovan's words, but the big woodranger, Tom Kearney, jumped into a boat and pushed her out from the slip.

' Arrah ! what is it to me where he lives, so long as he pays me me wages ? Hurry on, boys !'

Half a dozen men scrambled in after him, and the boat was away into the darkness in a moment. A contagious thrill of excitement ran through the rest ; there was a rush for the slip, a hustling and crowding, and, without quite knowing how or why he got there, Rick found himself in the stern of the long lobster-boat, with her tiller in his hand, steering her through the swarm of little boats moored off the pier.

The lobster-boat was low in the water from

the number of men who had crowded into her, but six strong fellows sent her along at a pace that soon lessened the distance between her and Kearney's boat. Rick was too much occupied for the first minute to think of who were with him, and after Donovan's loud protests on the pier, he was considerably astonished to hear his voice close to him.

' Ye shaved Cat Island Point that close ye'd think ye were in as big a hurry as Tom Kearney,' he said. It was too dark to see his face, but Rick seemed to hear a sneer in the husky voice. ' Pull away, boys !' he continued ; ' I'd be sorry Tom beat us, and we'll all have a dhrop of something betther than wather once we're done with the fire.'

That it was a big fire was evident. The quivering glare became each moment more vivid, and when they rounded the second point, there was a weird flush on the rough black water ahead of them.

' It must be in the back o' the woods down by Scariff,' said Rick, trying to keep out of his voice the anxiety that was growing in him.

' Well, with this wind the river will stop it,' answered Macarthy, who was pulling stroke, turning to look at the sky; ' but I think meself 'tis north of the woods entirely.'

They were now close on the third point, and the trees on the high shoulder of the hill were silhouetted against the fiery clouds. There was a shout from the leading boat, and the rowers in both slackened.

' It's not the woods at all!' shouted Tom Kearney ; ' it's the Widow Leonard's house!'

The words turned Rick blind and giddy for an instant, like a blow, and in the next had stimulated him to a kind of madness.

' Row !' he yelled, springing to his feet. ' What are ye stopping for, ye fools ?'

The boat swung round the point, the men

staring in amazement at Rick's agonized
features as he stood facing them with the
tiller in his hand and his eyes straining
ahead of him, till the full light of the blaze
fell on them, and with one accord all turned
towards it.

The fire itself could be only imperfectly
seen through the trees scattered along the
banks of the Rowrie, but Rick could make
out something that looked like a black gable
from which the lurid smoke and sparks went
streaming away down the wind.   Donovan
burst into a peal of falsetto laughter.

'So that's what we were killin' ourselves
to get to! The Widow Leonard's chimbley
afire! Ho, ho, ho! Well, boys, afther that
I think we might as well come about, and
get that dhrop of dhrink I was talking about.'

There was no mistaking the meaning of
his brutal indifference.   Rick turned on
him, reckless of what he said or did.

' Ye lie !' he said fiercely. ' Ye know well
that's no chimney ! Isn't it enough for ye
that ye have them near ruined without
leavin' them to burn, ye cowardly hound ?
Pull on, men—for God's sake, pull !'

Dinny Macarthy put his oar into the water,
but none of the other men stirred. There
was another cackle of laughter from Donovan.

' I thank ye for yer language to me, Misther O'Grady,' he said, raising his voice so
that the men in the other boat could hear ;
' it shows yer fine breeding. Well, boys,
he's a great commandher, and he thinks he
can ordher us all about as if we were black
slaves, but I'd adwise ye to mind yer own
business, and let him and his commands go
to the divil.'

The fire gave a stronger leap into the sky ;
by its light, Rick saw the broad face of his
enemy looking up at him with a coarse grin,
and his voice shook with rage and despera-

13—2

tion as he made his last appeal to the open-
mouthed, listening men.

'Is it *him* ye're afraid of? what sort of
cowards are ye that the likes of that skunk
has ye all under his thumb?   I tell ye 'tis for
his own reasons he has that woman boycotted, and not for the sake o' the League!
I tell ye no harm at all 'll happen ye if ye'll
come ashore with me now and lend a hand
to help those poor creatures; sure, boys, ye
wouldn't see an old neighbour in danger and
leave her in it!'

The wildness and intensity of his expression transfigured him as he leaned
towards them, but there was no response
to his passionate appeal; only a ghostly
echo babbled and hooted it back to
him from the darkness of the wooded hill
opposite.

Donovan seized the tiller and pushed it
hard down.

'Give way, men,' he said ; ' we've had enough o' this.'

The oars went in with a splash at the bidding of the gombeen man, and the boat lurched jerkily round.

' P'raps Misther Richard O'Grady——'

Without waiting for the end of the sentence, Rick put his foot on the gunwale, and sprang from the boat far out into the water. They saw him rise a good ten yards away, and an irrepressible ' Bravo !' or two mingled with the sound of the water in his ears as he swam with all his strength for the Point.

CHAPTER XV.

OUT OF THE DEEP.

ELLEN LEONARD was very tired that Thursday night when she had finished the last of her many tasks and subsided beside her mother into the mountainous feather-bed that was a monument to the many geese who had sufferingly yielded its substance from their living breasts. She was so tired that in a few minutes her overwhelming sleepiness swathed itself soothingly round the new keen happiness and anxiety that were shut up together in her heart, and for an hour or more she slept without a dream, without a stir.

Then slowly some glimmer of waking life

reached down to her in the black well of unconsciousness. She realized that some familiar sound was recurring again and again, and in some way appealing to her. The thought of morning came struggling into her mind, and quite suddenly she found herself broad awake listening to the cocks crowing, loud and shrill, in a shed outside. She turned herself towards the little window; there was a ruddy light in it that she could not understand. 'Sure it couldn't be morning yet,' she said to herself. Something like a falling star drifted past the window, another and another followed ; then she started up, trembling all over, and, calling loudly to her mother, leaped out of bed and rushed to the window.

The hayrick at Scariff was built at some little distance to the west of the house, standing commandingly on a small rocky rise in a corner of the wide field in which most of it

had grown and been made.   It had been burning for more than half an hour before Ellen
saw it, and by the time that she and her
mother and Dan had hurried on their clothes
and rushed out to it, the flames were tower-
ing above its black ridge, and bending before
the west wind in stupendous banners of fire.
The sparks fell thickly round the three as
they ran through the clouds of stinging,
pungent smoke, and when they neared the
great glaring furnace, the muffled roar and
the heat became so dreadful that even the
widow's breathless curses and bewailings
were terrified to silence.

Gasping and choking, they made a wide
circuit to the windward side of the hayrick,
and there, with the wind fanning the murky
heat away from them, they saw the full extent
of the disaster.   Half at least of the winter
provender of the widow's cattle was already a
mound of glowing ashes, and the other half

was being rapidly devoured, with a horrible soft crackling sound, by the flames that the wind was driving into its heart.

'Wather!' shrieked Mrs. Leonard, waving the bucket that she, like Dan and Ellen, had snatched up as she left the house; 'throw wather on it! Oh, God help us! God help us!'

'Wather!' replied Dan hoarsely; 'ye might as well be spittin' on it! if ye empt'ed the well on it itself, 'twouldn't save it.'

'Oh, but look at the stack of sthraw,' exclaimed Ellen; 'the sparks is coming to it already!'

The stack was a low round one, standing partly in the lee of the hayrick, so that every now and then the trailing sparks were swept over or past it. As Ellen spoke, a little wisp of burning hay drifted on to it, dying as it alighted.

'Oh, Lord save us! did ye see that?' she

cried. ' Hurry, hurry, Dan ! maybe we might get the wather from the well that'd save it.'

She ran down the field towards the well in its furthest corner ; and the widow and Dan followed her. Journey after journey they made ; running down the rough slope with the empty buckets clanking, staggering up the steps of the well, and back again across the field, the precious water splashing out of the buckets at every unguarded step ; and then the moment came that seemed so inadequate after all the toil, when the paltry bucketful that had cost so much, and was worth so little, was flung on the stack. Sometimes they were forced back by a whim of the wind sending a sickening, scorching gust of smoke in their faces, and the sparks would fly round them like a swarm of fiery gnats, and each time as the smoke lifted they expected to find the dreaded spot glowing in the stack. But each time as it cleared they saw the sparks hissing into blackness on the wet straw, and they felt encouraged to persevere. At last the widow gave in ; half-way to the well she collapsed on to the grass.

'O God!' she cried, 'I'm owld and wake. But yez that's young and has the strength, go on while yez have it. O mother of God! Oh, the bloody villians!'

They left her there, moaning and crying and clapping her hands, and ran on to the well. Ellen's breath was coming in thick gasps, and her knees trembled under her as she groped down the dark steps of the well. Dan had got there before her, and she heard him scooping the water into his bucket with the bowl that was kept in the well for times of drought.

'Go back, Ellen,' he said ; 'there's not half the full of a bucket left in it. We're done for now entirely.'

The little vault of the well gave his voice a
hollow and fateful ring, and Ellen sank down
on the steps above him.

'The well dhry!' she said in a whisper;
''tis too much misery we has to bear! I wish
I was dead out o' this.'

He left his bucket in the shallow water,
and came and stood on the step below her.

'Is it wishin' yerself dead y'are? There's
others is as mis'rable as yourself, and worse,
and not a word of pity ye have for them.'
He put his hands on her bent shoulders:
'Look up at me now; don't ye know that
ever since I was a little gossoon I was aimin'
to marry ye; ye knew that well, and ye
never said agin' it, and I was damn sure that
comin' on next Shraft we'd be marrid.'
Excitement had given him a power of words
that was very unusual to him, but here his
breath was caught by a dry sob. Ellen
looked up and saw his broad face working

and quivering, and his light eyes holding the
flare of the fire in them like a dog's.

'Dan,' she said, a sick chill of terror inter-
weaving itself with her despair, 'don't talk
that way, for God's sake ; come out o' this ;
it's no good for us to stay here. Come on.
Why ! we must do what we can to save the
stack.' She tried to get up, but his great
hands pressed her down, and he went on as
if she had not spoken :

'I declare to me sowl I was glad when
they boycotted us ; I thought, surely ye'd
see then how 'twas for the sake of yerself,
and nothin' else, I stopped on here. 'Twas
little I thought ye'd turn about and threat
me like the dirt o' the road.'

'Ye know I never done that, Dan,'
faltered Ellen. 'Ye know I always had a
great wish for ye, and we were always
friends that way.'

'Ye lie !' he said, with such fury that she

shrank away with a terrified cry. 'If ye
had any wish for me, ye'd not take up with
the worst enemy yerself and yer mother ever
had—him that's makin' a fool of you, and a
beggar of yer mother, for the sake of Donovan's wife!'

Ellen struggled to her feet with something
of her mother's spirit roused in her.

'He thinks no more of Harriet Donovan
than I do!' she said, with no smallest
tremor of uncertainty in her voice; 'and
I wouldn't care if everyone livin' was down
on their knees tellin' it to me. I wouldn't
believe that Rick O'Grady ever done a hand's
turn agin us!'

'There's one that maybe ye'd believe without she goin' down on her knees to ye,' retorted
Dan; 'and she could tell ye that he was only
here to do her husband's business — and
there's what his business is!'—he flung his
hand out towards the burning hayrick. 'Ellen,

I'll never sarve ye that way!' She was standing on the step above him, and he suddenly threw his arms round her waist with a hoarse cry of rage and despair. ' I'd sooner see ye dead than married to him !'

Ellen had one glimpse of the face that was so near to hers.' There was a stare like madness in the eyes, and she shrieked as she tried to tear his long arms asunder.

A light so fierce broke on them at that moment that every stone and blade of grass was lit up, and before she could realize what it was, she found herself free. She turned and faced, as Dan was facing, towards the hayrick. Its eastern gable, undermined by fire, had toppled over in one huge burning mass on to the stack of straw, and the flames were spouting up like the waters of a fountain, Ellen saw between her and the blaze her mother's figure, with wild arms waving above her head, and she ran towards her, scarcely

noticing that Dan made no further effort to
stop her.   Had she looked at him, she would
have seen that his eyes were fixed on a man
who was running fast across the field towards
the hayrick ; but she saw only her mother's
despairing figure.   She never looked back
as she sped along the wet path from the well,
and she was thus spared what would have
been for her the culmination of that night of
horror.   Dan had fallen forward on his face
upon the slimy steps of the well, and was
lying there, breathing stertorously, with foam
upon his lips.

The widow saw Ellen coming, and ran
distractedly towards her.

'Come home, come home, ahudth !' she
wailed.   'It's all disthroyed on us, and we
might as well go undher the sod, for they'll
burn the house over us next!   Mother of
God! who's this ?' she shrieked, suddenly
falling on her knees.   'They're comin' to

murdher us altogether ! Run, Ellen, run !'

But Ellen had seen as soon as her mother the supposed murderer, and seen him with such a flood of joy in her heart, that she had no voice to call to him. She stumbled towards him with outstretched hands, and before Mrs. Leonard's appalled, incredulous eyes she fell into his arms and laid her head on his shoulder.

He was bare-headed and all breathless from his run, and the sea water dripped from his clothes.

' I couldn't save your hay,' he panted, ' but, thank God, I saved your house and your cattle. And what signifies the hay so long as you're safe yourselves ? What signifies anything——

His voice failed him, but it may be presumed that Ellen heard the rest of the sentence.

14

Amazement had so far relaxed the tension of Mrs. Leonard's nerves that she had sunk from her knees into a sitting position on her heels, but the most supreme emotion had never been known to deprive her of her power of speech.

'Let go me daughther, ye bloodthirsty villain! Isn't it enough for ye to ruinate and disthroy us this way, without tellin' lies that's as black and as bloody as yer own heart!'

She shook her two clenched fists in the air at the rescuer.

'I came near losing me life to get here to help ye,' said Rick, in a voice that carried conviction with it; 'and if I hadn't come, ye wouldn't have had a roof over yer heads to-morrow. I found James Mahony on the pigsty wall setting a light to the thatch of the cowhouse, and he's lying there now in the ditch under it, with his leg broke.'

CHAPTER XVI.

HUSBAND AND WIFE.

FRIDAY morning was dark and wet. The
south-west wind had not failed of its usual
custom, and Dinny Macarthy had spoken
truth when he told Rick that rain was near at
hand. But in spite of the heavy sluices that
darkened the heavens over Rossbrin, and
raced in yellow rivulets down its steep street,
the stir of a delightful new excitement was
perceptible in all its pulses—that is to say,
its public-houses.

Every man had his own version to give of
the scene of the night before, and still more
abundantly had every man his prognostica-

tion as to what would come of this quarrel
between the two leading luminaries of the
place. Rick O'Grady had been seen very
early that morning driving in the direction of
Cloonmore, and not long after his return, Mr.
Donovan had set off in the same direction.
These important facts having been discussed
in all their bearings, it seemed certain to Rossbrin that 'the gombeen' had gone to swear
'informations' against Rick for libel and
abusive language, and whatever the latter's
business might have been, it seemed pretty
certain that in one way or the other, the
quarrel would afford the pleasurable excitement of a day in the Court House at Cloonmore.

It happened, however, that Donovan's
object had been rather to seek information
than to impart it ; but it also happened that
he had been unsuccessful, and at about half-
past two o'clock he was nearing Rossbrin, no

wiser, except in a negative sense, than he
had been when he started. He had made
inquiries at James Mahony's lodgings, and
was told by the harassed, good-natured
mistress of the house that Mahony wasn't in
all night, and that, indeed, it was a quare
thing for a man to lave his child that way,
and only for herself giving him his breakfast,
the creature'd be lost with the hunger.
Donovan gave her a shilling, and departed,
the unpleasant truth now forced upon him
that his ally had got into trouble of some
kind. He knew very well that the Rossbrin
sergeant of police must already have made
inquiries about the burning of the hayrick,
but as President of the Land League, his
diplomatic relations with that officer were a
trifle strained, and his guilty conscience confused his power of deciding whether it would
be advisable to consult him on the subject.

His temper was not at its best, when cold,

wet, and hungry, he got back to his house;
and the conditions there were not calculated
to soothe a man in his then frame of mind.
On the table of the sitting-room an uninviting
lump of half-cold pork surrounded by a dark
and flabby heap of cabbage was waiting for
him; the fire was nearly out, and a half-
empty plate showed that his wife had not
paid him the compliment of postponing her
dinner on his account. The ill-humour
darkened in him as he bolted his unsavoury
meal. 'How bad she was that she couldn't
wait a half-hour for me!' he thought resent-
fully as he rose to get the whisky out of the
cupboard by the fireplace. 'And why
couldn't she come in here while I ate me
dinner, without leavin' me by meself this
way?' He knelt heavily on one knee to
unlock the cupboard door, putting one hand
on the narrow wooden upright of the chimney-piece to steady himself; and as he did so,

a stick that had been leaning in the corner
by it fell clattering on to the floor in front of
him. Donovan picked it up. It was a
smart blackthorn with a silver band, and he
did not need to read the letters R. O'G.
engraved on the band to tell him whose it
was. 'What the devil brings his stick
here?' he said to himself, getting on to his
feet. 'It couldn't be he was here yestherday
evening afther she tellin' me last night he
wasn't when I axed her about him.' His
face reddened all over, and his fingers
clenched on the blackthorn till his hand
trembled. He went to the door, and calling
the girl from the kitchen, asked her where
her mistress was, and hearing that she was
'above stairs in the hotel parlour,' he went
straight up there, with the stick still in his
hand.

Harriet had betaken herself to the rarely
used hotel sitting-room, ostensibly to arrange

and dust its desolate decorations; but her duster was lying clean and folded on the dilapidated keyboard of the little old piano, and she herself was standing in the window, looking vacantly out into the rain, that in the last hour or so had degenerated into a thin drizzle. Her hands knotted and unknotted the blind cord restlessly, while her thoughts spun in an endless circle round one centre— that stormy interview with Rick; and no matter how often she thought of it, her pulses would give the same throb as she lived over again the moment of farewell. It had meant everything to her: confession, promise, seal, the old passion reawakened on his part, the new justified on hers. During a sleepless night, and a long solitary morning, she had fed her heart with these thoughts, and now at length excitement and the uncertainty of her hopeless and yet irrevocable love wrought her up to the pitch of tears, not blinding and abundant, like those she had shed last night, but of the slow-trickling and agonizing kind.

Her husband's voice speaking to the servant recalled her to herself. Her eyes were dry in a moment, and when he came into the room she was languidly dusting the clinking glass pendants of the candlesticks on the mantlepiece. She took no notice of his entrance, and the big man stood silent for a moment or two, certain of his purpose, but irresolute how to enter upon it. At last :

' Harriet,' he said, ' didn't ye know I'd come in ?'

' Yes, I did,' she answered, without turning her head.

' Well, I think ye might have seen that me dinner was hot for me, so,' he rejoined, blustering a little so as to overcome a latent fear of her.

To this he received no answer, and after
a slight pause he cleared his throat.

'Did ye get any news while I was out
about the business at Scariff last night?'

'I suppose it's the burning of the
Leonards' hayrick ye mean?' replied Harriet
indifferently. 'I'm not in the habit of going
out looking for news, and as ye said nothing
to me about it, I didn't ask any questions.
It was Joanna had some talk about it. Is it
Captain Moonlight again, I wonder?' There
was a faintly mocking tone in her voice, and
she turned her head a little to see how her
husband took the insinuation.

He changed countenance slightly.

'There's no believin' the talk these people
have,' he said; 'I'll walk over meself in the
coorse of the afthernoon and see about it.'

Donovan had not thought it desirable to
tell his wife any of the details of his last
night's adventure, feeling that she already

had more information about his affairs than
was good for her. He had thought much
and uneasily about Rick's accusation in the
boat, and now Harriet's elaborate indifference
seemed to confirm his suspicions. She had
been the traitor, and he held in his hand a
proof of her treachery.

'Was Rick O'Grady here at all yestherday?'
he asked carelessly, but in the mirror above
the chimney-piece Harriet saw his face alert
with sinister inquiry.

'No; I know nothing at all about him.'

Donovan drew from behind his back the
hand in which he had been holding the
stick.

'Then I suppose I may take the liberty to
ax what brings his stick in my house?'

Harriet turned very pale.

'I suppose he left it the last time he was
here.'

'I'll swear that stick wasn't in the room

yesterday morning,' replied Donovan, coming a step nearer, his small eyes sparkling with the fury that was scarcely perceptible in his voice; 'I'd have seen it at dinner-time when I went for the whisky the way I did to day.'

'What's it to me where it was?' replied Harriet insolently. 'There's many a one of your friends comes in and out here unbeknownst to me!'

He came close to her, and, catching her by the arm, swung her roughly round face to face with him.

'I'll have no more lies from ye. Was he here last night, or was he not?'

'Let go my arm!' she exclaimed; 'ye're hurting me.'

He relaxed his hold, but did not let her go.

'Answer me that, now : was he here?'

'Ye needn't roar at me the way the

servant 'll hear ye,' she said, becoming malevolently cool and steady : 'as ye're so anxious to know, he *was* here ; and he heard ye kindly ordhering James Mahony's supper before ye sent him out to——'

Donovan cut her short with an oath.

'If ye say one other word' he said in a low voice, 'I'll put ye out into the street, and there isn't one but will know the reason why I do it !' He dragged her forward a pace, and then flung her from him with the full thrust of his arm. 'If I done right I'd beat ye with this stick the way I'd beat a dog,' he said deliberately ; 'but I b'lieve if onst I began I wouldn't stop till I killed ye.'

She felt for the first time the dread of his physical strength, and stood silently there, white-faced and panting, with her eyes fastened on his face.

'What did ye tell him last night about James Mahony ?'

'Nothing!'

'I suppose that's another lie!' He spoke
with a difficulty that told of mental torment
as well as rage. 'I suppose ye've told me
so many lies already, ye think another makes
no differ.'

'I told him nothing,' she said again; 'he
knows nothing but that James Mahony was
here.'

'Ye needn't throuble yerself to tell me
what he knows,' retorted Donovan. 'He
knew enough to come sneaking to my house
when I was out, and to run and hide in the
dark like a rat when I come in!'

The fire came back to her eyes.

'He didn't hide! He was standing looking
at ye, and for the matther o' that, it was *I*
asked him to come here!'

With a movement incredibly swift for so
cumbrous a man, he struck her across the
body with Rick's blackthorn.

She caught at the piano to save herself from falling, and a thin confused jangle came from its yellow notes, and mingled grotesquely with her cry of pain and terror.

Her husband stared at her, as if trying to realize what he had done, and then he broke the stick across his knee with one strong effort, and dashed the pieces down at her feet.

'There!' he said, 'ye may give him his stick the next time he comes here, and tell him the use I had for it; but I think I'll be apt to see him before you do, and to put him in a way that he 'll not be goin' visitin' again for awhile!'

'Do yer best, ye cowardly brute!' she said, with her right hand pressed to the place where he had struck her; 'it's easy to sthrike *me*, but I dar' ye to lay yer finger on *him!*

She was desperate at last, and she flung the taunt gallantly at him.

. He glared at her, and she at him for a few tense, dangerous seconds; then he made a kind of plunge towards the door.

' My God Almighty !' he said thickly, ' let me out o' this before I kill her——'

The door banged behind him, and a minute or two afterwards she heard his step in the street below.

CHAPTER XVII.

A WOLF IN A TRAP.

TORTURE—a shivering numbness, and a partial insensibility; then torture renewed a hundredfold, while unskilful hands jerked and dragged and lifted him. Another wave of sick faintness when he found himself stretched at last upon hay and pillows, and after that long hours of darkness following each other like blind tormentors, before James Mahony saw the dim wet daylight creep through the holes in the door of the shed in which he lay. As the light strengthened he looked about him at the bare stone walls, and realized to the full all the ignominy of his

15

position. Caught, and crippled, and disgraced, with nothing to look forward to but the prison infirmary, and dependent, meanwhile, on the charity of his enemies, the man who had slaughtered his neighbour's heifer and burned her hayrick was in as miserable a plight as the severest moralist could desire for him.

He closed his eyes and lay there, enduring as best he could his pain of mind and body, and listening with fevered anticipation to every sound outside while the gloomy morning wore on. Ellen came to him once or twice with food and drink, looking almost as white and exhausted as he did himself; but he neither looked at her nor thanked her. Soon afterwards came the worst moment of all, when the door was flung open by the widow, and he saw the tall great-coated figures and dark helmets of two of the Rossbrin constabulary in the doorway. Their visit was not a long one, nor did they gain much information by it, beyond that which Mrs. Leonard was volubly anxious to bestow on them. James Mahony told them his name, and where he lived, but beyond this he would answer no questions, and his broken leg served him as a temporary protection from further terrors of the law. Then they went away, and his lonely suffering was unbroken by any incident for another hour or two. He guessed it must have been about noon when he heard a quick footstep outside, and then the widow's voice in excited questioning from the cottage door.

'Are they comin' for him ? I didn't look to see ye back for another hour. Were ye in Cloonmore at all ?'

The old man started erect on his couch of hay to hear the answer.

'I was, to be sure!' answered Rick O'Grady's voice. 'I got Hennessy's car in Rossbrin, and I wasn't long on the road.'

'Throth, and ye were not! But tell me now, what's to be done at all?'

Fortunately for Mahony, the closing of the yard gate, always a complicated matter, kept Rick outside, and enabled him to hear the answer to the question.

'They can't send for him at all to-day. The hospital van was gone out ten miles the other side of Cloonmore, and so I said ye'd keep him till to-morrow. I went to the doctor then, and he said he'd be out here before night. I hope he'll not be late, for I have to be back at home before the eight o'clock mail car goes out.'

'And what about the summons?' The widow's voice sank on the last word, and the straining eager ears of the listener could just catch the reply as Rick crossed the yard.

'I didn't go to the Cloonmore police at all: I thought I'd thry could I get anything out of the old man himself first. I think there's others——'

The end of the sentence was lost in the shutting of the cottage door, and after that there was silence for a long time, except for the monotonous drip and patter of the rain, and the disconsolate crooning of the hens under a cart in the yard.

The doctor was better than his word, for it was still daylight when his trap rattled up the lane and he presently came into the shed with Rick O'Grady. The agony was short, but while it lasted Mahony never opened his lips to complain ; nor when the strapping and binding of the broken leg was ended did he make any sign of relief or gratitude. The dispensary doctor had seldom had a patient of this kind, and his eyes wandered curiously over the long gaunt figure as he gave Rick his orders as to the treatment of the case.

'You can move him into the house now if you like,' he said finally.

The patient fixed his hot suspicious eyes upon the doctor. 'I'll not be stirred!' he said. 'I'll stay where I am.'

'Oh, please yourself!' replied the doctor, buttoning on his mackintosh, too hurried to argue about a trifle; 'if you like hay better than blankets, I don't care ; only keep quiet wherever you are.'

When he was gone, Rick came back into the shed.

'What way does the leg feel with ye now, Mahony ?' he said not unkindly.

Mahony turned his head away.

'I don't know what way it is,' he muttered sullenly.

Rick looked down at him uncertainly, with his hands thrust deep in his pockets, and at last sat down on the side of a furze-cutting machine that stood near.

'Well, I'm sorry it was through me ye were hurt that way,' he said. 'I never got such a surprise as when I seen it was you I was afther knockin' into the ditch.' He waited to see if Mahony would speak, and then went on: 'But what's more surprising to me is that a decent man like you would go put his hand to such work as that to spite an old neighbour. I'd bet twenty pound this minute that there's more than yerself in the business.'

Mahony turned his head towards him.

'Ye're very smart,' he said slowly, with the pant of pain still in his voice. 'And ye think ye have me under yer fut now, but I'll anser no questions to plaze ye.'

'Maybe it'd be better for ye if ye did,' said Rick, standing up; 'but that's no affair of mine. There'll be more than me asking ye questions before they're done with ye.' He walked to the door, but there stopped again.

'Come now, Mahony,' he said persuasively, 'who was it set ye on to do it?'

Mahony heaved himself on to one elbow.

'*Hon o maun dhiaoul!* Will ye lave me alone?'

He had his wish; the door was slammed and Rick came near him no more.

Exhaustion had her way at last. While the meagre light in the shed dwindled and dwindled with the dying day, Mahony fell into a doze which deepened into a heavy sleep. It was quite dark when he was awakened by loud voices in the yard, and for a minute or two he did not take in things sufficiently to distinguish whose they were, till a movement on the part of the speakers brought them nearer to the shed.

'I know as much of the League as yerself,' said Rick O'Grady's voice. 'And I have it in black and white that this boycottin' is no work o' theirs.'

'If ye knew anything of it, ye'd know it
was its business to put down land-grabbing,'
said the voice that Mahony was somehow not
surprised to hear. 'And if there's outrages
ensoo, that can't be helped——'

'Oh, curse it all!' broke out Rick, 'what's
the good of wasting time picking me words
for the likes o' you? What I say, and what
I'll stick to, is that you, and no one else, is at
the bottom of this business. I saw that last
night in the boat; and, what's more, I say that
James Mahony was acting by your orders.'

'Ha, ha! ye doublefaced villain! Answer
that, ye mane blagyard!'

It need scarcely be said that this inter-
polation came from the widow.

'It's little use talkin' to them that won't
listen.' Donovan's voice was as coolly
deliberate as ever. 'But I may as well tell
ye, Misther O'Grady, that ye'll get no good
of thryin' t'intimidate me, and that ye're liable

this minute for an action, for accusin' me of
being a party to the outrages of that old beg-
ging thief.   I'd tell him to his face, if I could
see him, that the sooner he goes to Cork Gaol
the betther plazed I'd be ! and if there was a
ha'porth I could swear agin him, I'd go into
the Coort to-morrow and give evidence.'

The listener in the shed clenched his bony
hands and groaned out an oath between his
teeth.

' Then perhaps at the same time ye'll
explain to the Coort what he was doing
sneakin' into yer house last night ?' The
accusing voice lacked somewhat of its first
energy and conviction.   There was a slight
pause, and when Donovan answered, his
voice was low and hoarse with passion.

' Sneakin' !' he repeated ; ' if it wasn't that
ye're the damnedest sneak in Ireland yerself,
and well ye undherstand what I mane, ye'd
not know so much about what goes on in my

house! Ye may make any story ye can out of
my givin' a bit to eat to a starving man that
darn't show his face to his creditors in
Rossbrin, but ye'll have to explain more
than ye'll care for before ye're done with it,
and ye'll have to begin with me this very
night—— That's what I come here for,
and I'll not go till I've done with ye; come on
out of this, away from these infernal women,
and I'll let ye know who's a liar and a sneak!'

A shrill torrent of vituperation from the
widow drowned Rick's reply, but the sound of
movement made Mahony guess that he had
assented. Then Donovan's voice again,
this time nearer the cowshed. Mahony
gathered himself for an effort as the footsteps
neared the yard gate.

'Open the doore!' he called out; 'open
the doore, till I spake to him!'

It was flung open immediately, and the
light from the wide-open cottage door,

opposite, was just enough to show him the figure of his late friend and employer.

'That's the man!' he cried, his voice sharp with weakness and rage; 'John Donovan's the man that done all this, and dar's to call me a thief now! I had his money, and I had his ordhers, and I'm a ruined man this night through him and his lies. 'Twas for himself he wanted the farm Drimnahoon, and I was to be his caretaker; deny that now, if ye can!'

He fell back in the hay, his head reeling from the exertion. Owing to this and the uncertain light, he could not see what happened next. Whether it was that Rick seized Donovan's arm at this, or that Donovan pushed the other roughly out of his path, but there was suddenly a struggle between the two men. Grappling together, they passed out of his range of sight; he heard the trampling of their feet through the shrieks of the women, a clang as of the shutting of the gate, and then Rick's voice loud and breathless.

' Go home now, and summons me as fast as ye like! I'm not afraid of ye, and I'll see that there isn't one in the parish but'll know the truth about ye by this time to-morrow !'

There was no response from the lane. Evidently Mr. Donovan thought that, after all, discretion was the better part of valour. James Mahony fell back again in his bed of hay, and felt that there was one pleasure that misfortune had not had the power to take from him—he had seen his desire upon his enemy.

CHAPTER XVIII.

THE place where her husband had struck her still burned and ached as Harriet left the hotel, and went quickly down the wet street in the twilight towards Rick O'Grady's house. She hesitated before she lifted the knocker, and then beat such a tattoo upon the door as brought Rick's old servant shuffling up at her best speed.

'Did Mr. Donovan call here?'

'He did, ma'am; he was here not half an hour ago, asking for Misther O'Grady; and I told him he wasn't here, and that he went up to Scariff afther he come back from Cloonmore, and he wouldn't be back here agin till seven o'clock to night.'

'And what did Mr. Donovan say?' said Harriet.

'He said, ma'am, "No matther," says he; "I'll go meet him there," says he, and he folly'd on then down through the woods.'

Harriet turned abruptly away, without troubling herself to make any further remark, and the old woman was left on the doorstep, full of unimparted facts and of indignation with Harriet for not waiting to listen to them.

It was nearly five o'clock now, and though the rain had stopped for a little while, the heavy clouds made the evening very dark. Harriet looked fearfully at the woods that stood like a black barrier in front of her; everything had its suggestion for her excited nerves, and the trees, crowding darkly together, seemed to be sheltering vague horrors, nightmares, that would creep whispering after her along the path. At another time she would have turned back, but that same excitement of the nerves proved itself stronger than its own tremors, and she went straight on into the wood. All about her in the gloom was the quiet ghostly drip from the wet branches, and the smell of decaying leaves rose rankly upon the damp air. Her ears were strained for the sound of footsteps, but the screeching and barking of the herons down in the tall firs by the shore, and the rumble of carts on the far-distant Rossbrin road, were the only noises that broke the stillness.

From what the old woman had told her, Rick must have met her husband by this time. The thought spurred her on, with always the second mad thought following on it, of how, when Rick heard from her of all that had happened, he would avenge her of that blow that his own stick had dealt her. She had lost her mental perspective; with the memory of that kiss still living on her forehead, nothing was impossible or improbable; everything had changed, and she was living in an agonizing, ecstatic world of blind hope and unreason. The darkness deepened about her, and when she came at length to the top of the slope that led down to the old bridge, the light in the Widow Leonard's cottage on the hill at the other side of the river twinkled distantly before her. She paused at that sight; it came like a full-stop to the rhapsody of her mind, and for the first time since she left the house she began to consider the practical side of her project.

The light had one meaning for her above all others; it was shining from the place where Rick was. She troubled herself with no questions as to what brought him there; she had long ago made up her mind that he

had taken the Leonards' part out of anta-
gonism to her husband and a high-handed
contempt for authority, and every feeling she
had was centred on the thought of seeing
him, and telling him all she had endured for
his sake. The rain had begun again, dropping sadly and heavily like tears of a grief
that is inconsolable. She made up her mind
quickly, as was her. wont, and went down
the path over the wet tufts of grass and
slippery sheets of rock, till she came to the
gaping doorway of the mill. A heap of
stones lay on its threshold, with the grass and
nettles growing up through them; she
stepped in over it, receiving a drenching
blow from the bush of ivy over the door as
she did so, and groped her way to the hole
in the wall in which the iron axle of the mill-
wheel lay in a paste of mud and its own rusty
flakes. The ivy grew like a tree on the top
of the gable, and protected her a little from

the rain; she knelt down on the old mill-stone that lay under the opening and strained her eyes into the darkness outside.

What she could see was only the black flood of the river beneath her, swollen high and fierce by the rain, and the slight outline of the bridge against the lesser darkness of the sky. The river was so full that it ran smoothly over the submerged rocks, except where a glimmering white gush of water showed here and there where some of the bigger boulders still lifted their heads above the swift current. She listened long and earnestly, and thought once or twice that she caught the sound of angry voices up at the cottage; but the waving and creaking of the trees in the freshening wind, and the noise of the water, made everything uncertain. She gazed at the cottage light till her eyes were tired, and changing her position, she put her elbows on the broken ledge, and rested her hot forehead on her hands, still listening intently.

She had remained thus for a few minutes, when a sound like the breaking of timber, followed by a slight splash, startled her. She looked towards the bridge ; there was a figure on it. It was too dark to distinguish anything beyond the fact that it was a man, and with the instinct of a person in hiding, she kept perfectly quiet. She heard again the wrenching and breaking of wood, a second splash and a third, just distinguishable above the roar of the river, and then the figure moved back along the bridge and went away up along the opposite bank of the stream.

Harriet scrambled to her feet and crept out on to the path again. There was nothing more to be seen or heard, and, after a second's hesitation, she stepped on to the bridge, and, with her hand on the rail,

advanced very cautiously a few steps.
Before she was half-way across she stopped
with an exclamation of terror. Right under
her feet the darkness moved ; it was the
water, ten feet below, that she saw through
a great gap in the timbers of the bridge.
The half-rotten logs had been torn from the
two supporting spars that spanned the stream,
leaving a space like a big open trap-door, a
space through which a man might easily fall
before he had time to put out a finger to
save himself. She looked down at the rapid
water in a kind of stupor ; she saw the
intention very clearly, but for whom was the
trap set ? and who set it ? There were just
then but two men in the world for her—the
man she abhorred, and the man she loved—
and of these one hated the other more than
anything on earth. These were her premises,
and with her husband's threats sounding in
her ears, the deduction was swift and sinister.

She crept back off the bridge and leaned against the wall of the mill, her knees bending under her from the shock. It was hideous! but yet, what better could she have wished than to save his life from her husband's treachery? She would call to him and stop him; she would tell him of the villainy that had been planned against him; he would know how true she had been to him. There was a footstep in the lane on the other side of the river. It came nearer, a footstep not like Rick O'Grady's, but heavy and uncertain. Then she heard a cough, unmistakable to her accustomed ear, and a clearing of the throat. It was her husband. The crisis of Harriet's life confronted her in one moment, and, to do her justice, her first impulse was to call out that there was danger ahead, but before her lips opened some devil's messenger of a thought shot luridly through her mind.

This was Rick's work; he had met her husband, he had heard disgrace and foul abuse heaped upon her, and for her sake he had taken this way of revenging her, and opening a door into a new life for her and for him.

Her husband's step was on the bridge; she became rigid and numb, and all things seemed as unreal as a dream. Then she heard a stumble, a cracking of wood as the hand-rail broke, and a horrible hoarse shout that was drowned in a splash below. A shriek that she was scarcely conscious of broke from her, and she rushed on to the bridge. There was nothing to be seen through the gap in its timbers except the strong black river — nothing to be heard except its flowing.

She turned, and, not knowing what she did, fled away through the woods.

CHAPTER XIX.

A SHAKE OF THE HAND.

THE rain fell at intervals till a little after midnight, and then with the turn of the tide the weather changed. The wind no longer drove the heavy clouds before it, and as the dark cold hours wore on it fell to a sigh, and finally there was a complete stillness. An hour before the late winter dawn the lethargy of the woods was stirred by the first mysterious breath of coming day, and the cocks crowed sleepily up at the widow's farm. Soon afterwards there fell from the uncertain obscurities overhead the faint harsh quackings of a string of wild-duck, coming from Corran Lake down to the sea, and a kind of grayness began to be reflected from the sky upon the mud flats in Scariff Bay.

The tide was dead out. The serpentine channel that the Rowrie River had worn for itself in the mud began to show more and more in the strengthening light, and the piping and whistling of the curlews and 'kilkeentra' awoke as if by magic all over the wide, palely-gleaming expanse. Tall ragged stakes that marked the channel at high water stood nakedly in the ooze, with the seaweed hanging in glutinous branches from them; and sticking out of the mud on the inside of one of these were the ribs of an old boat, that had gone to pieces there years before, and now, matted over with seaweed, was the most chosen home and nursery for crabs and fat mud-worms. As a rule, it was at low tide the centre of a screaming,

squabbling party of birds, but on this bitter
November morning, while the gray streaks
of light lengthened in the sky, each bird, as
it alighted at the accustomed spot, lifted its
wings again, and skimmed away to find its
breakfast elsewhere.

A narrow strip of land, known as Scariff
Point, ran out southward into the mud to
about fifty yards from the boat.   There was
a low scrub of furze-bushes on it, and a few
wind-dwarfed fir-trees, and between these,
just as the first thin rays of sun stole over
the crest of the hill eastward of Scariff, Dan
Hurley came running.   He was quite breathless, and he stumbled two or three times
among the furze-stems, but he kept on without a stop till he had scrambled down to the
water's edge.   He sat down on a rock there,
and dragged off his hobnailed boots, and
tucked his trousers up above his knees.   He
was so exhausted that he could scarcely get

up again ; he had not slept since Ellen's cry
of fire had awakened him the night before
last, and the last time he had eaten anything
was nearly twenty-four hours ago, when,
after lying out in the field all night after that
seizure at the well, he had slunk into the
house for his breakfast, and gone out again,
no one knew whither.   He himself was now
beginning to forget how he had spent his
day : things were narrowing in about him in
some strange way, leaving nothing clear but
his present object.

He had spent a long night of excitement,
wandering about the Trahartha woods, and
with the first gleam of day he had gone
down to the river bank to see whether the
tide had or had not begrudged to him the
sight of his victim.   There was nothing
in the river; he followed it down to its
mouth, and there was nothing there.   But
even in that faint light he saw, as he looked

out across to Scariff Point, something that
sent him running at full speed, scrambling
back across the perilous broken bridge, and
on among the gorse and trees till he got to
the Point.

He had changed very much in the last
two days. His face was flabby and blue,
and his bloodshot eyes had a stare that was
almost vacant, and yet had some wild
purpose in it. He climbed feebly over
the weedy rocks, and, plunging his bare feet
into the deathly cold mud, began to make
his way across it towards the old boat. He
had often waded about in the mud of Scariff
Bay, to get worms for bait, and now,
though he sank to his knees, he went
steadily on. The thing that he was making
for lay in a shapeless heap up against the
ribs of the boat, just as the last lift of the
falling tide had left it. As he neared it
there was something about it that puzzled

him. Rick had been wearing a light suit of
tweed when he saw him last, and this soaked,
huddled-up object was all dark ; besides, it
looked heavier and thicker. He made
what haste he could, though the exertion
was dreadful, floundering on through the
blue-gray mud that softened and deepened
as he neared the channel of the river, and
then at last he saw his work and its
failure.

There was little of John Donovan's face
to be seen, as he lay with his head plunged
into the rank tresses of seaweed, and a
big nerveless hand and arm sprawling out
over the mud. Dan stood staring at him,
the hatred of a lifetime almost forgotten
in unutterable amazement and disappointment, his teeth and hands clenched, and
the blood banging and hammering in his
head. What had brought Donovan up to
the farm last night ? Dan cursed the rest-

lessness that had driven him away from that
safe hiding-place at the back of the cowhouse, where he had lurked when he saw
Rick coming up the lane, and where he had
so successfully, as he thought, overheard
his plans.   If he had been content to wait
there he might have known all about
Donovan or anyone else who went to the
farm.   Well, it was no harm done, any way ;
he had had it in for him this long while.
It occurred to him then that the situation
was ludicrous, quite enchantingly so, in fact,
and he began to laugh in loud peals that
lifted the sea-birds from their feeding-place
in squealing, fluttering rings, and roused the
echoes in the hills.   The echoes seemed to
amuse him too ; he listened to them and
laughed back to them till he was exhausted.
After all, it was a fine stroke of luck that had
put one of his enemies out of the way ; he
would go back now, and patch up the bridge :

not securely, of course, but so that he could set his trap again to-night and catch another big rat in it.

The thought nearly convulsed him again with laughter, but he knew that he had no time to waste. He stooped forward and took John Donovan's stiff hand in his.

'Well, good-bye to ye!' he said; 'maybe ye'll be out in the harbour's mouth before night, and I mightn't see ye agin.'

He tried to shake the hand up and down, but it felt as heavy as lead. It seemed to him as if it were pulling him down; blackness came before his eyes, and he screamed, or thought that he screamed. But the hand still drew him down, and he fell forward and lay, face downwards, in the mud.

There was great quietness after this, and before long the startled sandpipers and curlews were hopping and running about, and digging their long bills into the mud, not twenty yards from where the two figures lay.

CHAPTER XX.

'FOR YOU I DONE IT.'

THE dawn showed itself later in Harriet's dark room than in Scariff Bay. While the sky outside was becoming gray and bright, the closed shutters and the paraffin-lamp prolonged for her a night that hours before had seemed endless; and even when a pale strip of light made its way in and fell upon her bent shoulders and dark, dishevelled head, she still sat on at the table in the yellow glow of the lamp, with her hands over her eyes, oblivious of the change.

Footsteps in the street made her lift her head at last, and starting up, she went to the window, opened the shutters, and raised the sash softly. She looked eagerly out, with eyes dazzled by the large mild light, and saw two or three fishermen coming up the hill. They were talking to each other in what seemed to her lowered voices; and as they passed the house she drew back a little from the window to listen. It was only something about their trade, after all—some discussion of a sleepy, interjectional kind about a neighbour's boat, —and Harriet put her head out again and looked down towards the sea.

She was still wearing the brown coat that she had on in the woods the evening before, and her hat lay on the undisturbed counterpane of the bed; while the mud about her boots and dress showed through what quagmires she must have wandered before she came into the house. She had told the servant, then, that she did not know where the master was, or when he would be in, and

had gone up to her room to spend the night
sitting in a chair, with her wet clothes drying
slowly upon her—sometimes shivering and
thrilling with nervous excitement, sometimes
becoming like a stone from the ghastly fore-
bodings that fastened on her. There were
moments when the reiteration of one idea
produced a kind of mental numbness, much
as the thundering of a train at night will, for
a short instant, seem to die in the traveller's
tired ear; but each space of insensibility was
bought by fiery awakening pangs, when some
sleepless intelligence lighted up the darkened
brain-picture, and the wet ivy touched her
cheek, and the logs were slippery under her
feet, and her husband's cry rang and rang in
the darkness.

The cold air at the window penetrated
through and through her, and leaving it,
she put out the lamp, feeling, as she did so,
that the night with its unrealities was over,

17—2

and that the daylight had brought her face to face with the practical consequences of her husband's death. Then she walked across the room and looked at herself in the glass. She saw there what might have been expected, a gray-white face with miserable black wisps of hair about it, and hot heavy eyes, and mechanically taking up her brush, she began to smooth her hair. Then another idea occurred to her. She changed her dress and boots, disarranged the bed so that it should tell no tales, and then lay down on it to consider her next move.

The servant was already moving about downstairs, and as Harriet listened to her singing at her work, and heard the cheerful ordinary sounds in the street outside, the agony of terror at what was to come caught her with a ruthless hand.

'Oh, Rick!' she gasped, with her face hidden in the senseless pillow, 'my darling

boy, I knew 'twas for me you done it, and I
couldn't hinder your work—but if they find
you out—oh, my God! if they find him
out——'

The fit passed off her again, and she lay
quiet and pallid on her bed till she heard
the clock below strike nine. She got up at
that, and putting on her hat and coat, went
downstairs. Michael was tidying and arrang-
ing the shop as she came into it, and she saw
him hang a bundle of blank bills inside the
railed desk, and put the pen and blotting-
paper ready for the hand that would never
use them again. The ground seemed to
rock under her feet, and for the first time
a faint whisper of remorse awoke in her,
but she walked steadily on out of the
shop.

A cold wind, with all the rawness of last
night's rain in it, struck at her as she went
down the street, and it, and the crude familiar

realisms of the shop windows, seemed to
take some of the white heat from her intention, and leave it shivering and feeble. She
met no one ; but down at the foot of the hill,
near the two trees, she saw a knot of fishermen, and as she crossed the street to Rick
O'Grady's house there came out of his door a
man whom she knew well—one Donaleen—
a purveyor of lobsters and crabs to the village.
He looked strangely at her, she thought, but
went down the hill without speaking to her,
and as she knocked at the door she saw him
join the group of men by the trees, who, she
now noticed, were all staring at her with unusual interest.

Something must have happened — they
must have found him. She had not expected it so soon, or in this way ; she had
imagined the messenger of death coming
to her house, but not to Rick's ; why should
they have come to Rick ?

'Oh my God!' she thought, 'have they found him out?'

She became aware that the door had been opened, and that Rick was standing before her.

'Come inside, Harriet,' he said in a low, agitated voice, taking her cold hand, and drawing her into the little sitting-room. He shut the door behind them, and then, turning white-faced to her, he said tremulously: 'When did ye hear it?'

She stood motionless, while Rick's dog, roused from its sleep on the hearthrug, jumped up at her, rubbing its head against her passive hand. Then, with a single cry of his name, she made an uncertain step towards him, and threw herself upon his breast.

'Don't say a word to me—I know it all!' she panted; 'I know that 'twas for me ye done it, my darling, darling boy! I was

waiting up at the bridge to speak to ye,
and I saw ye break it down, and then—
and then I heard John coming. Oh!
Rick——' She broke off, sobbing hysteri-
cally; 'he struck me yesterday with your
stick—I was comin' out to tell ye—and I
heard him—I heard him——'

Rick caught at her circling arms and tried
to unloose them from his neck.

'What are you talking of, Harriet? Are
ye gone mad?'

'Don't be afraid of me, Rick,' she went
on, in her infatuation clinging closer to him
than before. 'No one 'll ever know ye done
it but me, and I forgive ye, Rick—I might
have stopped him before he got to the
bridge, but I knew they'd never find ye
out——'

'What are ye sayin' to me?' said Rick,
with all the horror that he felt in his voice
and face; 'is it that yer husband was knocked

off the bridge and that ye think I did
it ?'

'Oh, I know it! I know it!' shrieked
Harriet, losing all self-control; 'who else
would do it but you, that hated him as I
hated him ? But they'll never know it,' she
repeated—'they'll never know it, and you and
me that loves one another will be happy in
the end.'

Rick tore her arms from round his neck
and started back from her.

'Let go of me!' he said roughly, while he
stared into her white, passionate face to see
if she were really mad or no. 'Do ye know
that yer husband's dead body was found
out on the mud at Scariff Bay, and Dan
Hurley's beside it ? It was Donaleen told
me that now, and I don't know what this is
ye're sayin' about the bridge—I never was
near it last night at all.'

She supported herself with one hand on

the table, and leaning forward, returned his gaze with an agonized intensity. Was this consummate acting on his part? or could it be——

'Rick!' she burst out, unable to bear the dreadful thought, 'don't say such things to me, or ye'll kill me! I'll not say any more to ye about last night if ye don't like. But, oh!' she went on desperately, her wonderful eyes melting and glowing, 'what's the need of secrets between us now? when ye kissed me two nights ago, then I knew ye were the same to me that ye were in the old days— and I was glad of the blow that he struck me— I knew ye'd revenge it on him——'

Rick turned away from her and groaned.

'It'll be all right now,' she went on eagerly; 'we'll——'

'Hold yer tongue!' he shouted, wrought from horror to disgust; 'have ye no decency in ye? I never saw yer husband afther he left the Leonards': we had words there, and more, and I'm sorry for it, but Mrs. Leonard and her daughter will tell ye I didn't leave the house till an hour afther he was gone, and I never was near the bridge at all—I came home in the punt, the way I went up. If anyone done any harm to him, it wasn't me!'

'Then who was it done it, if it wasn't you? I saw ye tear the logs off the bridge and throw them in the river—I'll swear it! I'll swear it!'

The miserable creature intended it as a menace, but even while she spoke her soul was dying within her. Rick did not answer for a few seconds, and when he spoke the excitement and protest were gone out of his voice.

'God forgive ye,' he said; 'and God forgive me, too, if anything I said to ye put ye asthray this way.'

The change in his voice and manner had
more effect upon Harriet than all his previous
denials. She put one hand over her eyes,
and stretching the other out in front of her,
made as though she would stagger to the
door, but swayed so helplessly at her first
step that he had to catch at her arm to keep
her from falling.

'Ye needn't be afraid of me, Harriet,' he
said, unconsciously repeating her words to
him; 'I'll not give ye away, ye poor un-
fortunate creature.'

She looked at him with dry, scared eyes,
and saw the tears standing in his.

'God knows I was very fond of ye once,
and ye wouldn't have me then,' he went on;
'and if ye hadn't changed to me, I'd never
have changed to you. But that's long ago
now—and——'

'Are ye goin' to marry her?' interrupted
Harriet in a whisper.

He knew what she meant, and he nodded his head.

She sank from his hand down on to the floor, and caught his knees in her arms.

'It was for you I done it,' she gasped almost inaudibly—'for you, that doesn't care if I was dead along with him!'

There was a sound of many feet in the street outside, a buzz of suppressed voices, and a crowd of people passed slowly up the hill, with, in the middle of them, something long and white, carried on a door supported by two long oars. He tried to move quickly between her and the window, but before he could do so she had seen what was passing, and catching at her loosened black hair with a gesture as though she would tear it out, she flung herself down with her face against the dusty floor.

CHAPTER XXI.

VOCES POPULI.

For at least a month the people of Rossbrin and its neighbourhood enjoyed a succession of the most satiating topics of conversation. John Donovan's death in itself, and under the most ordinary circumstances, would have been a social cataclysm of highest importance, but shrouded and, as it were, embalmed in mystery, it took a place far above anything that had before occurred at Rossbrin.

That Dan Hurley's body should have been found in inexplicable companionship with that of the man whom he was known to hate gave such a final touch of the marvellous as

almost to stagger the receiving capacity of
the parish, and complicated the otherwise
obvious suggestion of the broken bridge.
The inquest was adjourned for some days in
order to take the affidavits of James Mahony,
and of Harriet Donovan, who, since the
morning when her husband's body had been
brought home, had been prostrated by a low
nervous fever — an illness that was considered by her friends a mark of admirable
taste and feeling. It had become known
that Mrs. Donovan had gone out to meet
her husband on the night of his death,
and had returned, wet through, without
having been able to find him, and had
gone out again the first thing in the morning to make inquiries about him. 'And
to think,' as Miss Vickery said, 'that the
first thing that poor creature'd see was
himself coming up the street drowned, and
she out on a fasting stummick ! It'd be no

wonder if she'd lose her life after the like
of that !'

But it was not from Harriet's statement
that the truth, or as much of it as was ever
known, came out. It was proved that John
Donovan had set out for Scariff at half-past
four o'clock, and from the evidence given
by the Leonards and Rick O'Grady, it
appeared that he had arrived there about an
hour later, the time usually taken to walk
through the woods. He stayed there about
twenty minutes, and there had been, the
witnesses admitted, a dispute, which had
ended in Rick O'Grady turning him out of
the farmyard. Mahony's affidavit was then
read, establishing the statement of the other
witnesses, that Rick had not left the farm
for more than an hour after Donovan. It
was clear that the broken bridge must have
been the cause of the latter's death, and
the presumption was that it had been de-

stroyed by someone who had watched his movements to and from the farm. Donaleen, the fisherman who had found the bodies, had seen footmarks leading from Scariff Point to the old boat, and a pair of boots, that the widow identified as Dan's, was found on the shore. The most important part of the evidence came last, when Mrs. Leonard swore that Dan Hurley had all his life had a grudge against John Donovan, 'and in throth, the poor boy and his mother had hard thratement from him, God forgive me for sayin' it of them that's dead!'

Mrs. Leonard at this drew her blue cloak about her with an air that implied her power of further revelation in the matter of Mr. Donovan's usage of the Hurleys, had she been so disposed. Further questioning at first elicited only the fact that she thanked her God she wasn't one to tell stories nor carry talk, but she subsequently was induced

to give an indication of Donovan's manner
of acquiring the Hurleys' farm.   Her further
statement that Dan had been in a strange
and morose state for two or three days
before his death, and that he had not been
seen since breakfast-time the morning after
the fire, left a sufficiently strong impression
on the minds of the jury.   In the end, however, a cautious verdict of ' Death by misad-
venture' was brought in in Donovan's case,
there being no direct evidence to point to
Dan Hurley as the breaker of the bridge ;
and the medical evidence, showing that the
latter's death was caused by suffocation
in the mud, during an epileptic seizure,
made the verdict in his case a simple
matter.

These things and many questions arising
from them were still red - hot under the
hammers of public dispute, when James
Mahony was well enough to be able to

stand his trial as an incendiary in the Cloonmore Court-house. The reader may be spared the details of this proceeding, interesting though it was to all those concerned. The Parnell Commission has made most people acquainted with the ways of Irish witnesses of every type, and the facts that James Mahony had to relate are not unprecedented in the history of Irish crime. He made a clean breast of it, sparing neither himself nor the late President of the Rossbrin branch of the League, and when he had finished and stood waiting to receive his sentence, everyone in the court knew how ingeniously Mr. Donovan had combined his political and private interests. James Mahony got off with a light sentence and a weighty exordium from the County Court judge, and he limped out of court with a stoicism that was creditable in an old man who had begun the world twice over, and

18—2

for the second time had been worsted in the conflict.

A full account of the proceedings appeared in the local paper, and was read in all sorts of places, and by all sorts of readers. The secretary of the League at X—— was one of those to whom it was least agreeable. In spite of his letter to Rick, he had not interfered in the Drimnahoon business, and now he did not attempt any vindication of his late ally. Boycotting was a thing more easy to start than to stop; and a touch of discipline would do no harm to Mrs. Leonard, who had at all events shown herself to be insubordinate. At a subsequent period, however, he had even more cause to regret that he had given Mr. Donovan a free hand, when he found out that certain money had been, to put it mildly, misappropriated by the late head of affairs at Rossbrin; and this painful fact, combined with a lack of enthusiasm

among the members now that the gombeen
man's personal influence was withdrawn, may
account for the retirement of Rossbrin from
political usefulness.

Another copy of the paper was read by
Harriet, far away from the scene of her
husband's death and disgrace. She read it
with scarcely a change in her white face, and
when she had finished, laid it down and
looked absently out into the dingy Dublin
street. The grocer opposite to her lodging
had sprigged his window with holly and ivy
in honour of the approaching Christmas
season, and before she was aware of it, the
ignoble decorations, in their setting of hams
and globes of lard, led her thoughts back to
the rank abundance of the evergreens in the
Trahartha woods. The illness from which
she had just recovered lay like some dark
cloud between her and the past, and the
mental agony that had at first seemed

unendurable had become a dull, everyday part of her life. But the vulgar reality of the newspaper, and the subtle suggestion of the green things, together gave her a pang that might have come from hell itself. This was her last day as a free woman, a creature of hopes and plans; to-morrow she was to become a cipher in a great system, and to sink into the anonymity which the Church of Rome offers to those who have found their own part in life rather more than they are able to play.

It may be doubted whether the —— Sisters of Mercy would have considered her a very suitable inmate for the religious quiet of their establishment, had they seen her, late on the last night of her liberty, kneeling at her bed-side, her remorse and penitence put by for a future day, weeping fierce unsatisfied tears, with Rick O'Grady's photograph pressed to her lips.

At that very time Rick was standing beside Ellen Leonard at the yard gate at Scariff, while the stars sparkled frostily in the dark sky, and the country quietness lay all about them.

' I'm not as good a chap as what ye think,' he was saying ; ' whatever I did for you was no hardship to me. There's things I can't tell ye ; but ye may believe me, I was to blame——' He stopped, and the hand that held hers relaxed its clasp and fell to his side. ' I'm not good enough for ye, Ellen asthore.'

Ellen's reply need not be recorded ; she was very young, and very much in love, and the pleasure of forgiving her lover was so new and exquisite that it cannot be wondered at if what she said was too incoherent to be submitted to the severities of print.

Whatever she said, and whatever he answered, it is certain that the widow, knitting away by the cottage fire, found that her patience was exhausted before the conversation came to an end.

' Come in out o' that, Ellen !' she screamed from the door. ' Don't ye know I'm bate out this minnit with walking Dhrimnahoon showing them bastes to the butcher—never welcome him to come the day Jerry was carryin' the mare to be shod! Go home, Rick, ye vagabone! Isn't it enough for ye that ye'll be marrid to-morrow? Oh, musha, musha! Them that's in love is like no one !'

THE END.

Ingram Content Group UK Ltd.
Milton Keynes UK
UKHW022211060623
422990UK00005B/136